Also by G.M. Malliet

The St. Just mysteries

DEATH OF A COZY WRITER
DEATH AND THE LIT CHICK
DEATH AT THE ALMA MATER
DEATH IN CORNWALL *
DEATH IN PRINT *

The Max Tudor series

WICKED AUTUMN
A FATAL WINTER
PAGAN SPRING
DEMON SUMMER
THE HAUNTED SEASON
DEVIL'S BREATH
IN PRIOR'S WOOD
THE WASHING AWAY OF WRONGS

The Augusta Hawke mysteries

AUGUSTA HAWKE *
INVITATION TO A KILLER *

Novels

WEYCOMBE

* available from Severn House

DEATH AND THE OLD MAST

DEATH AND THE OLD MASTER

G.M. Malliet

SEVERN HOUSE

First world edition published in Great Britain and the USA in 2024
by Severn House, an imprint of Canongate Books Ltd,
14 High Street, Edinburgh EH1 1TE.

severnhouse.com

British Library Cataloguing-in-Publication Data
A CIP catalogue record for this title is available from the British Library.

ISBN-13: 978-1-4483-1472-0 (cased)
ISBN-13: 978-1-4483-1538-3 (e-book)

All Severn House titles are printed on acid-free paper.

MIX
Paper | Supporting
responsible forestry
FSC® C013056

Typeset by Palimpsest Book Production Ltd.,
Falkirk, Stirlingshire, Scotland.
Printed and bound in Great Britain by TJ Books,
Padstow, Cornwall.

Praise for the St. Just mysteries

About the author

Agatha Award-winning **G.M. Malliet** is the acclaimed author of three traditional mystery series and a standalone novel. The first entry in the DCI St. Just series, *Death of a Cozy Writer*, won the Agatha Award for Best First Novel and was nominated for numerous awards, including the Macavity and Anthony. The Rev. Max Tudor series has been nominated for many awards as have several of her short stories collected in anthologies and appearing in *Ellery Queen Mystery Magazine, Alfred Hitchcock Mystery Magazine,* and *The Strand.* She was a graduate student at the universities of Cambridge and Oxford and now lives on the East Coast of the US with her husband.

www.gmmalliet.com

Acknowledgments

Once again, many thanks to my agent, Mark Gottlieb of Trident Media Group; Michael Pintauro, also of TMG; and the team at Severn House, in particular Martin Brown, Joanne Grant, Mary Karayel, Tina Pietron, Sara Porter, Rachel Slatter, and Piers Tilbury.

And to the experts in many fields who patiently answered my questions and allowed me to draw on their expertise, with special thanks to pathologist Dale Steventon and to the development team at St Edmund's College, Cambridge. All mistakes or misstatements of fact are my own.

And as always, to Bob.

'The aim of art is to represent not the outward appearance of things, but their inward significance.'

— *Aristotle*

Cast of Characters

- Sir Flyte Rascallian, master of Hardwick College, University of Cambridge
- Beatrice Rascallian, widow of Sir Flyte's uncle, Finneas Rascallian. Beatrice gives Sir Flyte a trove of papers and paintings from her attic.
- Detective Chief Inspector St. Just and Detective Sergeant Fear of the Cambridgeshire Constabulary's Serious Crime Unit
- Constable Abelard of the Cambridgeshire Constabulary
- Portia De'Ath, lecturer at the university's Institute of Criminology, crime writer, and St. Just's fiancée
- Dr Pomeroy, police pathologist
- Ambrose Nussknacker, curator of a small private gallery and museum in Cambridge. He wants to assess Sir Flyte's paintings – or rather, have a computer assess them.
- Barnard LaFarge, reporter for the *Cambridgeshire Bugle*. His story on a 'treasure trove' of paintings forces Sir Flyte's hand.
- Professor Patricia Beadle-Batsford, head of the university's Department of Women's Studies
- Peyton Beadle-Batsford, her rebellious daughter
- Rufus Penn, a twenty-three-year-old graduate student and Peyton's boyfriend
- Franklin Penn, Rufus's grandfather
- Mr Oliver Staunton, Hardwick College night porter. He swears he wasn't asleep when the crime was committed.
- Ms Zola Blaze, Hardwick College day porter and Oliver Staunton's confidante
- Mr Aled Evans, Hardwick College afternoon and evening porter
- Professor Annalise Bellagamba, Portia's colleague and an expert on art theft and forgery

ONE
Master of None

The dreaded call from Beatrice, eighty-five years old and finally moving into care, was an unwelcome reminder of how quickly time passed. If the indestructible Beatrice was succumbing to old age, surely his own demise was just around the corner.

Sir Flyte had a soft spot for his uncle's widow and knew he was overdue for a visit. Consulting the National Gallery on an upcoming exhibit of Old Masters had taken up much of his attention in the past year. He had let other obligations slide, although he dutifully telephoned Beatrice once a month.

The calls on his time as an art expert were becoming more frequent, and while his success enhanced the prestige of the college, being master of Hardwick College was his main job, along with writing books and delivering the occasional lecture to art history students. Everything else was a sop to the ego.

He did try to resist calls from museums and auction houses to weigh in on their planned acquisitions, but he rarely succeeded in stifling his curiosity. He liked being good at his job, bustling off to London or staying at a stately home, being plied with champagne and dinner after weighing in on the merits (or not) of a work of art. Being hailed as a hero when he was able to pronounce an artwork authentic or – more often – saving someone from spending thousands of pounds on a work of doubtful value.

Both guilt and affection compelled him this early September day to put aside these worldly distractions and drive the old Audi to Beatrice's house in the country. With the weather cooperating, offering a shimmering sun, white clouds, and a sustained light wind, he found he was enjoying the drive and looking forward to his visit. Of course, it would be tedious work helping her pack things in boxes and organize what was going into storage, which was most of her belongings. He had dressed for the job in what was, for him, casualwear: neatly pressed khakis and a button-down shirt with loafers.

Her accommodation at Elderwood wouldn't allow for the accumulated goods of over fifty years of marriage to his uncle, let alone the detritus of her career as a writer of children's books. That would be the hard part: helping her decide what could go and what could stay. Much of the physical work, packing the contents of shelves into boxes, must be left for the removers due to come the following week. Copies of all of Beatrice's published books were going into storage, along with a few treasured volumes she didn't trust to her new situation.

He was, he supposed, her sole remaining heir, and what he was meant to do with them all – well, he would cross that bridge later. He doubted they were worth as much as she thought they were.

She had put off calling him for help until the last minute, when the sheer amount of work became overwhelming. This was typical of her – even with her health quickly fading, her first concern was 'not to be a bother'.

She lived in what had been the manor house for Lower Snaverton, the original village that time forgot, nearly a two hours' drive from the Master's Lodge. If there ever had been an Upper Snaverton it had long vanished from modern maps.

The village was closer to being a hamlet, but for having a church, which elevated it to village status. It was connected to the main road by a single rutted strip of macadam, but there were no intersecting roads, no further entrances or exits. Once you were in Lower Snaverton, if you found you didn't like it, you had no choice but to turn round and go back the way you came.

The journey took him through the beautiful Fen country. Many people found the Fens bleak, flat, uncompromising, and rather boring, but Sir Flyte had always felt something about the stark isolation of it all matched something within him. Not that he was stark and bleak, but that he felt in his bones his ancestors had seen this identical landscape. The Fens were a tie to the past. *His* past.

Sir Flyte was all about the past. He was an expert in the Old Masters and, apart from a handful of Impressionists (excepting Gaugin; he detested Gaugin, both the man and his work), modern art interested him not one jot. His expertise had carried him into a place of honour as master of Hardwick College at the University of Cambridge. He could hardly believe the title himself, let alone the 'Sir' before his name. His father, if anything, had been anti-intellectual, a commercial traveller who was all about hail-fellowing and business deals. In his absence, amidst his many disappearances into pubs 'for work', his mother had been the one who made sure there were books on the shelves and galleries to visit and plays to see. Many of their weekend outings included visits to museums, which was of course where he met the love of his life: Rembrandt.

Ahead he saw the turnoff for Lower Snaverton, and slowed the car for a left turn. Over the years there had been more traffic build-up than could be believed, but once he was off the main artery and passing the ornate sign for the village with its unlikely coat of arms, the familiar landmarks presented themselves. He was surprised the dress shop had hung on, a bastion of flowery tweeness in a world long moved on to latex and Internet shopping. The post office had closed a decade before, along with the butcher, but the tea shoppe, which looked like something that might have been mentioned in the Domesday Book, was still operating.

One woman, clearly a customer of Viola's Dress Shop, was visible in the window as he drove by. She didn't bother to hide her curiosity at this rare visitor, and she waved energetically to him as he passed. He supposed his aunt had told the village of his impending arrival. It only took one person to be informed for the whole village to know.

Of course, there was a pub, the Queen's Arms, not yet open for gossip. And a church, St Michael's in Glory, limited now to saving souls every other Sunday when the priest they shared with nearby villages came to town.

'He's like a gunslinger in an old Western film,' Beatrice had told him. 'Dropping in every other week to keep the peace.'

He felt at ease as he drove, as comforted by these sights as if this were a homecoming, although his real home of origin was London.

As soon as he reached the edge of the village proper and saw the house, he was taken aback. It looked deserted – as if it had been deserted for some time. It was evident that nothing had been done to keep the place tidy. The garden was overgrown. A shutter hung loose at one of the windows. The brick path had sprouted weeds, and the flowers that could be bothered to bloom that summer had wilted and now lay where they had fallen.

There being no drive up to the house, he parked the Audi by the gate opening into the walkway. The gate, like the shutter, hung by one hinge, and that hinge was red with rust. Beatrice had been expecting him, but he supposed anything like tidying up for visitors was beyond her now. Besides, she would be leaving soon. It did beg the question of who was going to buy a house that looked as if no one had ever cared about it.

He sighed. If Beatrice planned to leave the house to him, he might have to oversee its being demolished, which would be a shame. But renovating even a small manor house circa the eighteenth century was a job for mad dogs and Americans with purses bursting with cash, and he couldn't imagine either wanting to live this far from anything.

When his uncle Finneas had been alive, everything had been tended to and tied back, weeded and deadheaded and fed with bonemeal. Gardening had been one of Finneas's joys, and while he lived any screw that needed tightening had been tightened. The sorry state of the roof alone would have had him spinning. He had been the very picture of a retired solicitor living in the Home Counties, reading the *Daily Telegraph* over his morning oatmeal and harrumphing at the decline in moral standards and the latest absurdity proposed by the Labour Party.

The door to the house inched open slowly as he came up the pathway, as if the heavy wooden door were being tugged at with a great deal of effort. He hastened his steps to help.

He had expected Beatrice to have changed, but the reality was startling. She had always been what might be called a full-figured woman, but she had lost about two stone and two inches from her frame since his last visit. Her appearance would not shock anyone meeting her for the first time, but of course he had years of memories to erase in an instant. Her eyes were clear, however, and despite her obvious frailty, they gleamed with an obvious delight at seeing him.

She leaned against the open door to admit him and he gently embraced her, afraid of breaking her ribs.

'Come in, come in,' she said. 'This is so good of you, Flytey.'

He only allowed her to use the childhood nickname.

'I'm only sorry it took me so long to get here,' he said. 'I've been remiss; I should have come sooner. How have you been coping?'

'Perfectly fine,' she said. 'I'm from a long line of women good at coping. They survived the war; I'll survive this.'

No need to ask what war. For her generation there was only one war. Even though she'd been a baby when it started, the war had taken away a father she'd never got to know. She had been sent to wait out the fighting on a farm in Wales.

She'd told Flyte once that she never felt the war was over until, when she was a teenager, rationing finally ended and she was able to buy a new hat.

'You'll see, you will thrive in your new place,' he said, doubting that could be the truth. She had often expressed the wish to die in her house alone rather than be surrounded by strangers.

'We know how to adapt,' she went on. 'It's just my legs, you see. My knees, ankles, hips – well, the whole works. Arthritis. I can't do the stairs anymore. I've taken over the dining room as a bedroom, but the parlour is still suitable for visitors. Come along.'

Entering the living room, he thought its suitability was an optimistic evaluation. The chaos of moving was clearly under way. Boxes had been unflattened and taped into squares and some books had been removed from their shelves, but that seemed to be the extent of the progress. What looked to be dozens of framed photographs and ornaments still needed to be sorted and packed.

He should have arranged to stay overnight; he would have to come back another time before she was finally moved out.

'Well, it looks like we have our work cut out for us,' he said.

'It's not as bad as it looks,' she said. 'The men are coming tomorrow, and they'll deal with it.'

'Tomorrow? You said next week.'

'They changed the schedule on me. Well, not them, but the care home said they had a sudden opening. I think we know what that means: someone died, probably playing croquet or following an altercation over the Scrabble board – so they had an opening, and rather than inconvenience them, could I move in sooner? I said yes. I didn't want to lose my place in the queue. It was hard enough to get a spot at Elderwood.'

'I see,' he said.

As he turned his attention to the books, she apologized for her slow progress, but one look at her hands told the story. The arthritis was pronounced. What had been a slight swelling of her thumbs had become a claw-like deformity of all her digits. If her feet were in the same condition, it explained her hobbling walk. She'd be in a wheelchair soon. Once again, he was awash with guilt. How had she been coping on her own for so long?

'Have you been able to get any help from the villagers?' he asked hopefully. 'From your friends at the church?'

'Oh, yes,' she said. 'Those boxes got assembled by Gracie from the choir, and the rest of them have been good about bringing meals and helping me with basic chores. Ralph from the post office, when we had a post office, offered to stop by and tend to the garden, but he hasn't got round to it yet. He's not well himself. The entire village is fading away, you know. The young people – there's nothing for them here. They all take off for London or Cambridge or Milton Keynes, quick as they can, although what anyone finds to do in Milton Keynes I cannot imagine. None of them seem to want to come back when it's time to start a family. Who can blame them?'

Who indeed?

'There's paper to wrap the few knickknacks I want to take with me.' She pointed one gnarly finger at a box of brown paper beneath a shelf holding the usual ceramic sheperdesses – sheperdi? – and flowers and animals. 'Oh, and before I forget, what I really need you to do while you're here is go up in the attic. I can't manage that ladder – quite impossible – but there are some paintings up there I know Finneas would have wanted you to have. Especially as you're an expert. I'm sure they're worth something, but you'll know better than I do. I insist you take them. I'm not putting those into storage to disappear. They meant too much to him.'

Inwardly, Flyte sighed. This was the danger of people's attics. Emotional boobytraps, every single one of them.

'How long has it been since you've been up there to have a look round?' he asked.

'Oh, ten years? Maybe more. Not since Finneas died. I would tell myself it had to get looked at, at least get someone up there to dust and deal with the cobwebs, but . . . you know. There were always other priorities. You'd be surprised how busy life can be in a small village, even Lower Snaverton. I shall miss it.' She held up one hand before he could speak. 'Don't say I'll make new friends. It's the last stop before you know what, so why make friends when you'll have to leave them soon?'

He thought there should be some anodyne response to this, but of course she was right. No use dressing it up. It was one of the things he loved and would miss about her, her complete lack of sentimentality, except when it came to Finneas. There, he was sure, memory had painted over quite a few of his uncle's flaws. He'd been twenty years older than his wife and a bit of a dragon, especially in his later years.

They set to work, Beatrice sorting books into piles, and he wrapping and boxing the breakables. She invited him to take what he wanted of those and he set aside a pair of moulded crystal candlesticks.

Around noon, a woman stopped by with a basket containing sandwiches and bottled ginger drink. This was Gracie from the church; he remembered her from previous visits. Gracie seemed to be, in contrast with Beatrice, doing very well. She, too, was shorter, perhaps by an inch – the village was shrinking in more ways than one – but she stood ramrod straight whereas Beatrice was showing signs of a dowager's hump.

She wouldn't stay to join them ('Women's Institute today. They're still fighting over the compost speaker. I'll come back and help if the row doesn't go on too long') but as she left, Beatrice turned to him and said, 'If you're going to go up to the attic, you'll need to do it before the sun moves too far behind the trees. It's dark up there – just a single bulb, and one small window. Right now would be the ideal time.'

He thought it interesting that she had memorized the changing seasons and the movement of the sun to such a precise degree, but of course she'd grown old along with the house, had moved here with her husband when she was little more than a girl.

He made his way upstairs carrying a torch she provided. The attic door was in the ceiling, the steps brought down by a rope. Nothing about it suggested that anyone had ever bothered to try the door for ages, and he was rather hoping to find it stuck permanently shut.

But tugs on the rope finally released the steps in a shower of fine dust. He was certain going up there would be like entering the Sahara. Fortunately, his job had had him crawling around enough attics in old homes that he had no fear of spiders and their webs, although a tarantula in a museum in Key West had nearly undone him.

When his head cleared the attic opening, he took a quick look around. The space contained the expected overflow of the years, masses of it. She had said the paintings she wanted him to retrieve were in a cabinet.

'It's in the corner,' she'd told him, a wooden cabinet meant to keep the dust off what were her husband's prized possessions. Flyte did stop to wonder why, if they were so prized, they were hidden away where no one would ever see them, but maybe that was the nature of hidden treasure. He found he was now curious to see what they were.

He pulled his weight up to a seated position on the attic floor, legs dangling over the side, holding the torch in his right hand. He was getting too old for this kind of carry-on.

He wished he were wearing some form of head covering and a lab coat. At least a face mask. He really should have thought of this beforehand. He stood upright on the attic floor with very little grace, swatting away as much dust as he could from his clothing.

He located the single light bulb she had mentioned and found it was working. His vision augmented by the torch, he was able to take in his surroundings more fully. The expected jumble of steamer trunks, disused chairs, spooky mirrors, and collapsed boxes met his gaze. In the far corner was the promised cabinet. It looked like it might be worth something to an antiques auctioneer. He'd have a word with Beatrice about getting someone in to appraise at least some of the things going into storage, if only for insurance coverage.

Pulling open the doors to the cabinet, he saw some old dresses and coats hanging from a rod, and beneath them several parcels wrapped in brown paper and tied up with string. Seven of them in total, he counted, as he pulled them from their hiding place.

One by one he carried them to the ledge of the attic door and from there down the stairs. They were small but Flyte didn't trust himself to carry more than two at a time.

She was still in the parlour, making fitful attempts to sort the books. It was clearly a painful process. She could only hold one good-sized volume in her hands at a time, and even that small effort made her wince in pain.

'I found the paintings,' he said. 'Shall we have a look?'

'Certainly, let's—'

There came a knock at the door.

'That'll be Gracie again,' said Beatrice. 'Why don't you just take them with you so we can get on with things? Finneas was keen that you should have them, and I'm glad to know they'll be in such good hands. If anyone will know how to judge them, it's you. As I recall there's one in there— Well, you'll see. I thought it was rather too good to be hidden in the attic, but Finneas's collections came to take over the wall space. That's all been set aside for the Harvest Fayre's "bits and bobs" table.'

Flyte recalled with a shudder the sentimental Victorian art that once had covered the walls. He walked to the front door to admit Gracie.

'Thanks so much for your help,' he said, showing her in. 'You've no idea . . .'

'Oh, but I do. But it's what she'd do for me. Tomorrow

we'll get some of the villagers in to supervise the removers and carry out the lot being donated to the Harvest Fayre. I'll soon get her settled. Don't you worry.'

The three of them worked companionably until night began to fall. Flyte tackled the kitchenware, putting it into boxes, ready for transport. As of tomorrow, the house would sit empty.

He was saying goodbye to his childhood. At the age of sixty-five, he supposed it was time. But why was it so difficult to face up to?

It was going on for eight when they had to stop, but much of the sorting had been done, and the removers would have to deal with the rest. They had spent a full hour putting colourful tags on bits of furniture to indicate their disposal – Oxfam, the Fayre, the rubbish bin – and highlight the items which were, in fact, going into storage.

Beatrice was clearly tiring. They'd found the brandy bottle and some juice glasses and had said good night to each other over a nightcap.

He forgot to carry the still-wrapped paintings to his car until Beatrice called out after him. He supposed he must take them. He could not see his way to a polite refusal – she already had a house full of mostly unwanted belongings.

At this point he was weary and had little curiosity left to see what was inside the parcels. Having remembered his uncle's taste in art, he'd lowered his expectations. He had a drive ahead of him back to the Master's Lodge and wanted only a hot shower to wash off the dust of the day's work.

He decided he would one day pick out the best of the paintings to keep as a memento of Beatrice's kindness, putting paid to another chapter in his life.

It was as he was finally taking his leave that she thrust an old briefcase into his hands.

'Papers,' she said briefly. 'I haven't had time to sort through them all, but you'll know what to do.'

He doubted that. 'Surely, anything private, you'd best—'

'I thought of leaving it with the solicitor,' she said. 'But you're family – all I've got now. You do as you think best.'

Rather than stay and argue the point he kissed her cheek, gave her a gentle hug, and took his leave.

TWO
Sir Flyte Disposes

The weeks passed and Sir Flyte was absorbed back into his normal routine. The latest influx of students had begun arriving for Michaelmas term, and again he marvelled at how they managed to be so much the same and yet so different every year. Their failed attempts at nonchalance, at being thought 'cool', were touching in their sameness, however.

They could not, any of them, believe their luck at being where they were, the hard work of getting there nearly forgotten.

There was one young man from somewhere in the vast wildernesses of America – upstate New York, the master thought it was – who stood out for his looks alone, but also because he seemed to regard his place at the college as no less than his due. Sir Flyte, immediately taking against him, looked up his file and saw he was Rufus Penn, a graduate student from Yale, twenty-three years old. He would be attached to the Department of the History of Art, reading under Professor Bailey.

God help him. 'Old Bailey', as he was known behind his back, was kiln-hardened by decades of drumming artistic discernment into young brains. No amount of bluster ever got past him. Flyte wondered how young Rufus would fare under his tutelage.

He thought he might keep an eye on young Rufus.

Beatrice's paintings – or rather, Finneas's – he'd tucked into a little-used cabinet in his study, where they sat forgotten, along with the briefcase. His expectations for the paintings were now so very low he hadn't given them a thought.

And as for whatever papers were in the briefcase, he imagined it would take hours to sort through them all before throwing most of them away as rubbish.

He'd visited Beatrice at Elderwood – dreadful name – to make sure she'd got settled in, and when she asked about the paintings, he'd not understood at first what she was talking about. He had mumbled something to the effect he was finding them quite interesting. He wasn't sure he'd fooled her.

'We never had them appraised, but Finneas thought the girl might be worth a bob or two,' she'd said.

'I'll have a closer look,' he'd promised.

Then came the day the awful news arrived: Beatrice had passed away that morning. She'd been sitting at breakfast with her new friends and had suddenly excused herself, saying she didn't feel well. An hour later a member of staff had found her in her room.

Her kind heart had simply given out.

It was a peaceful death, they kept telling him, and he supposed that was a mercy, but once again he had failed to visit her as often as he'd intended, and once again he was plagued with regret and remorse that she'd died alone.

Part of his reluctance to visit, he knew, was a cowardly dread of seeing someone once so beautiful and vibrant diminished by age. Not just because her condition reminded him of his own mortality but because, in his own stilted way, he had loved her very much.

And – being honest – because all his life he'd loved beautiful things and shied away from the ugly.

From reality, his father would have said.

The funeral service took place in Lower Snaverton, well attended by the few remaining friends who lived there and presided over by the priest he'd come to think of as the gunslinger, an elderly man with a reedy voice and a black cassock shiny with use and smelling of tobacco smoke.

She'd left Flyte the house in her will, and he spent some time on the afternoon of the funeral with an estate agent to see about putting it on the market. Despite his fondness for Beatrice, he had few ties to the village and no use for the house. He supposed he might donate it to the college – perhaps they could use it as a retreat for scholars working on their dissertations and desperate for quiet and solitude.

But much better to lay the memories to rest, once and for all.

The sad day prompted him to think about digging out the paintings Beatrice had given him – that other, final gift from her and her husband. He felt obliged to dispose of them correctly. If there was a way to auction them off, if they had even the smallest value, he would arrange it. He certainly had the contacts for it.

He returned to the college late that night under dark autumn clouds thick with rain, too saddened by the day's events to deal with anything further. The next morning, however, he went directly downstairs and into his study, took the paintings out of the cabinet where he'd left them, and began removing their brown wrappings.

The first six were uniformly appalling – all unsigned, and rightly so, he judged. Two appeared to be family portraits and thus of limited value to anyone not directly related to the Flytes. He realized, not for the first time, he was the end of a long line, having never married despite a few near misses. But even he could see no earthly reason for holding on to portraits that documented the family's long red noses, small eyes, and bushy eyebrows.

The seventh painting was more promising. No doubt it was the girl Beatrice had mentioned. He set it aside for the moment. Perhaps the briefcase contained some documentation.

He found it locked. No key, of course, and a cheap metal hasp. He prised it open, ruining the lock, and began rummaging lightly through the contents.

He was still pondering what to do when Ambrose Nussknacker found him the next day.

Ambrose appeared just as Flyte was starting to put away the briefcase. Flyte resented the interruption, but because it was Ambrose, he waved him in.

'What in heaven are these?' said Ambrose. 'Not your usual line, I'd have said.'

That was certainly true. The family portraits had the look of works that had been done by someone with failing eyesight to record for posterity the general unsightliness of the Flytes.

Even Sir Flyte had to admit that while he'd been gifted in the brains department, nature had given him features that could kindly be described as distinguished. These two looked to be a married couple and one could not help but think they had been made for each other.

There was a painting of a horse, badly proportioned and standing awkwardly on uneven legs in an acid-green field. Two Fen landscapes, not terrible but amateurish, and what looked to be a country picnic scene that looked set to dissolve into an orgy before it was over.

Finally, a portrait of a young woman. A young woman with rather a bold stare, dressed in the fashion of the seventeenth century in a black gown with lace collar and cuffs. It was impossible to assess properly, given the grime and the fact someone had unhelpfully layered dark varnish over the painting at some time in the past, turning what had no doubt been white lace to grubby yellow. It also had been overpainted by a distinctly amateurish hand and, most unhelpfully of all, given a signature: Rembrandt. It looked to Flyte like a modern-day copy of a Rembrandt, although no such original painting existed in the accepted oeuvre of Rembrandt.

'No, you're quite right,' said Sir Flyte. 'Not my line at all.'

'Still, the one of the young woman . . .' Ambrose began.

'Yes, that's the only one that shows anything like value, given a proper cleaning. I would say fifty pounds at most. It would cost far more than that to remove the overpainting.'

'You say that without examining it closely.'

'You did interrupt me as I was getting ready to do so.'

'Here, let me at least look at the back of it.'

'I'll do that,' said the master rather abruptly, Ambrose thought, as he would later tell the police. It was unlike Sir Flyte to be so jumpy, so on edge. So rude.

It did make Ambrose wonder, he said, what it was about the painting that seemed to disturb Sir Flyte. For the master was an established expert in the field of art assessment. If he said something was worth fifty pounds, it was worth fifty pounds.

But as Ambrose told the police, it was the *way* he'd said it. It was more to get rid of him, Ambrose felt.

He described stepping back, stiff with offence, from the table where Sir Flyte had laid out the paintings, and meekly looking over the master's shoulder as he handled the paintings one by one, examining their backsides, as it were, before dismissively setting them down on the table. He did linger over the painting of the girl, holding it up to the light, but he didn't so much as use a torch or loupe to examine it. He flipped it over and looked at the mounting.

'The frame might be worth something,' the master said at last. 'Gilded eighteenth century. It's hard to even feel sentimental value for it, but I believe I'll hold on to this one a while. Feel free to take the others if you like.'

'I rather think I won't,' said Ambrose, now deeply affronted. He and the master went back years and he could not begin to understand why this collection of paintings troubled him so much. He agreed that all but one held little promise, so being offered the privilege of hauling them away to the rubbish tip was hardly a compliment.

'Are you going to have it assessed by another expert?'

Now it was the master's turn to be offended. 'I *am* the expert. And I can see at a glance this is not what it pretends to be.'

'A Rembrandt, you mean,' said Ambrose.

'I wouldn't even say from the school of Rembrandt. Nor a school run by his half-witted second or third cousin.'

'We won't know unless it's submitted for X-ray and the usual testing of the wood it's painted on and the paints themselves.'

'I know that,' the master snapped, 'and that's why I'm not bothering.'

'I'd be glad to take it off your hands along with the others, if that's the case.'

'No.' Sudden, abrupt, and final.

'We're doing some marvellous things with artificial intelligence these days, as you know,' began Ambrose. The 'we' was a mistake, perhaps, elevating himself to the lofty heights where the master dwelt nearly alone among highly sought after experts in the field of art assessment.

'Artificial intelligence will never, I repeat never, replace human intelligence when it comes to the field of evaluating rare paintings. A computer simply cannot do what the human eye can do and it never will be able to.'

Although Ambrose might have agreed in theory with this sentiment, he felt the master was using it to divert him from the topic of this one painting. But he decided to bow to the inevitable.

For now. The master was in no mood to be rational. The death of his aunt probably had unsettled the man. Maybe he'd try later.

Or maybe he'd approach the problem from a different angle.

THREE
The Night Porter

A week later

M r Oliver Staunton, the night porter of Hardwick College, thought he heard a shout at midnight, coming from First Court. A cry of some sort. He couldn't be sure because the college's chapel bells pealed out simultaneously, overriding what he thought was a human sound.

He listened intently in case the sound was repeated, turning up the volume on his hearing aids. He didn't think too much about it. Surrounded as he was by people in the full flood of youth, many of them free of the bonds of family oversight for the first time, there was little that surprised him anymore. But this was odd because that kind of carry-on normally came from Third Court where the first-years had their rooms. There were rules against loud parties and noises at that time of night, but it took a few warnings to get them all under control. High spirits, that was all, but rules were rules.

Oliver lived and died by rules.

He thought this noise was much nearer to hand, but he couldn't be sure. He'd been distracted waiting for a promised phone call from his grandson, a call that never came, and he'd allowed himself to sink into a bit of a funk, turning over in his mind what he might do to draw Gerry closer to him. He'd sent money for his birthday, a generous sum of three hundred pounds, but he'd got no thanks for it. From that abyss of failed bribery, his thoughts led to what he might have done wrong over the years to make the boy avoid him.

The job he was in, always surrounded by youth, was a painful reminder, although he supposed he should have welcomed them all as substitutes to help fill this hole in his

life. Every young man he saw with a certain gait, a dark
ponytail, or a pair of eyes to match his own made him wish
young Gerry had applied himself a bit more so he could mingle
with these sons and daughters of privilege. Nowadays that was
possible, if you wanted it badly enough. In his day it had been
the army or the mines. Coming up to Cambridge to study
wasn't even a dream, even if he'd had the qualifications for
it.

He'd been on the job since ten o'clock – those were his
hours, ten at night to six in the morning – so when he heard
the cry, he was two hours into his self-pity stage and entering
his worry phase. It didn't help that to stay awake he drank
large amounts of coffee from a flask, so any pretence of calm
acceptance of his fate had gone out the window by eleven.
And with all the coffee, he'd have to take frequent loo breaks,
besides.

It was really a job for a younger man, and he knew it, but
with the wife gone off years ago, he couldn't stand being stuck
in an empty house all day doing nothing. It wasn't in his nature
to do nothing.

He just wished he were more of a reader or a crossword
puzzler, needing something to pass the time and keep him
alert, because once the students were all settled in their beds,
there was little to do or watch on the telly in the small sitting
room of the Porters' Lodge. There was so seldom anything of
interest appearing on the security camera displays that he rarely
bothered to glance at the screens.

Still, the sound was out of the ordinary and he thought he
may as well go and check, even though it was probably that
American bloke with his girlfriend. It generally was. She
needed to keep a lookout, he thought. Rufus Penn didn't strike
Oliver as ready to settle down, and at his age, who could
blame him? But as the daughter of the head of the Department
of Women's Studies, the girl was putting her mother in an
awkward spot. Oliver realized that was probably the entire
point and besides, there was no love lost between him and
Professor Beadle-Batsford, but still.

With a sigh and a glance at the three security screens – still
nothing afoot there – he put aside the ham and cheese sand-

wich he'd bought from Sainsbury's for his midnight snack. He'd only managed one bite before the chapel bell tolled.

On reflection, the sound was coming from much closer than Third Court. And it didn't really have that shriek of ecstasy he was used to hearing from the American's rooms. He hoped those two hadn't decided to branch out, taking their love to another court or even up to the rooftops. If so, a stop to that would need to be put. A word in the master's ear should do it.

But in fact, the cry he'd heard sounded nothing like that at all, and in his heart he knew it. It was a sound he hadn't expected to hear again once he'd left the army. The sound of someone taken by surprise, someone in some sort of pain or distress.

A shriek of pain, followed by a sudden silence.

He struggled to his feet, grabbed his coat and the torch, and went to see what was up.

Locking the Porters' Lodge behind him, he stepped into the soft autumn night. It was time to lock the college gates for the night, but he decided to leave it for his return.

It was mild for the time of year and he quickly realized he needn't have bothered putting on his heavy woollen coat. He walked in the direction of the Master's Lodge because that was where he'd decided the sound must have originated. The master lived in solitary splendour in First Court, which also held the chapel and administrative buildings like the Bursar's Office – empty at night, of course.

Oliver reached the Master's Lodge with its weathered stone arches framing the entrance. He knocked hard at the iron-hinged wooden door. Receiving no response, he knocked louder. He did have a key, but he was hugely reluctant to use it. What if Sir Flyte woke up and asked him what he thought he was doing?

After a few minutes with no response, however, Oliver hauled the key ring from his belt and found the sixteenth-century iron key – not the original. That would have been fourteenth century.

But then he realized he needn't have bothered. The door

was unlocked and was in fact standing open a fraction of an inch.

It creaked open to his push with a loud screech – he'd have to get maintenance over to oil those hinges – and he eased his way inside, hoping the noise would alert the master to his intrusion. The hallway was dark, as the stained-glass windows admitted no light.

Every inch of panelled wall was hung with banners and coats of arms and relics of the college's history. Everywhere were paintings of Hardwick College's masters going back centuries – a parade of antique costumes and extravagantly bearded old sages – and recent photographs of gowned worthies smiling and shaking hands with visiting dignitaries. In one photo, Sir Flyte stood proudly with the then-Prince Charles. In another, he shook hands with Theresa May.

The lodging was like a small manor house, for in fact that was what it had been. It was much like the nearby Master's Lodge at St John's College, only older and smaller – its smaller size never mentioned, its antiquity a matter of pride. The colleges were nothing if not competitive, and it seemed to him that the smaller the issue, the more competitive they became. He supposed that friction was what made them throw off so many bright sparks.

Oliver knew that to his right was a drawing room, and behind it the master's study. To his left, the dining area. At the back of the lodge would be the kitchen, upstairs the bedrooms. He'd never entered either area. It was not much different in layout from the two-up two-down he'd grown up in, and yet was much larger and modernized and a world away.

They'd done away with the servants' quarters and expanded the living space some years before. It was a large space for a single occupant, but then a master needed space for entertaining those dignitaries.

Sir Flyte's bedroom would be upstairs. Oliver stood at the foot of the stairs calling his name. No reply. If possible, the silence was deeper than what Oliver would call a normal silence. The master kept no pets; there was nothing living to disturb.

Why had he thought that? Nothing living? When he himself

had seen the master that evening returning to his lodgings, hale and hearty – well, hearty for him, his nose pink from the earlier chill of the night. They'd exchanged greetings in passing, the master just bustling in as Oliver was taking up his post at ten.

Even if the master had gone out of the college again for some reason, he would have had to pass the Porters' Lodge both going and coming. There was no guarantee Oliver would see him, of course. He would be in his sitting room behind the reception area with the telly on, but at that time of night? No. The master was a creature of habit. He stayed in most evenings unless he was dining at another college. There was nothing to send a man his age back out after ten at night.

The master was here in his house. Logic dictated the master *had* to be here. Oliver started up the steps, calling, 'Sir Flyte?', still feeling he was making an unforgiveable intrusion into a superior's space, for Oliver was a rank-and-file man to his fingertips.

But something was wrong here, and he had entered enough buildings in Iraq and Afghanistan to be able to sense when there was no longer an active sniper, and any other occupants were likely dead.

The master's being dead wasn't impossible, he supposed. He and Oliver both had reached the age when every backache and chest pain and fleeting moment of vertigo was a potential heart attack.

Oliver reached the landing and stood quietly, wondering which direction to go. He decided to approach the first door off the landing. It opened into what he assumed from its size and grandeur to be the master's bedroom. Nothing there, nothing disturbed; in fact, the bed not slept in. He headed down the hallway, opening doors as he went. Nothing.

Now what? He must have missed something below.

Having hobbled back downstairs, he headed for the master's study, opening doors as he made his way to the back of the house.

At the third door he found him, sprawled across his desk. Quite still, not moving.

The green-shaded desk lamp was on; it appeared as if Sir

Flyte had been working late. Whatever he'd been writing, the pages were scattered, and some were littering the floor. A pen had fallen from his hand and spattered ink on the page. Ink dripped from the desktop where the bottle had been knocked over.

After seeing so many dead and wounded, Oliver didn't have to check for a pulse but out of habit, he did. One look had told him CPR would be useless. There was little blood left in the body for the poor man's heart to circulate, even if it could be resuscitated.

The size of the bloodstain on his back was proof enough Sir Flyte was dead.

Again, out of long habit, Oliver paused to say a brief prayer for the repose of the master's soul, then left without touching anything more.

Best leave this to the authorities.

FOUR
The Long Arm of the Law

Detective Chief Inspector Arthur St. Just was used to being wakened in the wee hours. In fact, over the years, he had become convinced that in the same way smoke detector batteries always quit in the middle of the night, crimes were never committed at any other time than between darkness and dawn.

He'd long since learned the art of the twenty-minute power nap when exhaustion inevitably caught up with him during the day. He could also sleep standing up in the incident room if that was the only option. But the fatigue seemed to be happening more and more often, and he wasn't even middle-aged.

A man in his forties was not middle-aged, he told himself firmly.

He'd said nothing to Portia about this tiredness, which he didn't regard as unusual. He was a police detective; of course he was tired. He was due for his annual check-up soon and might mention it to the doctor. Or not.

From the dark came Portia's voice. 'I'm so sorry, Arthur,' she said, lifting her satin sleep mask from her eyes. 'But the third time this week?'

'There's been a spate of armed robberies lately. I suppose someone's been harmed in the commission.'

'Are you this short-staffed?'

'Yes. At the start of a new term, there's a certain amount of commotion until everyone calms down. An assault can be anything from a pub bust-up to a murder, and a theft can mean anything from a bicycle to a work of art.'

He would come to know how uncanny those words were.

'This might end up being a case for Serious Crime – or not,' he added, heading for the bathroom. 'If bodily harm is involved, I'm involved. The night porter at Hardwick College called it in. They're treating it as a suspicious death so I'm off to see what's what.'

'Who is it?'

St. Just turned back at the door. 'It's the master, I'm afraid. Even more reason to step softly and quickly.'

'Not Sir Flyte?' She pulled the bedcovers closer to her body. 'Are they sure? Well, I guess the porter would know, but . . . Sir Flyte?'

'Do you know him?'

'Mainly by reputation. I have a colleague in the Institute of Criminology who consults with him often. She lectures in art theft and forgery.'

'And what's his reputation?'

'Impeccable. It's not possible for someone like that to be murdered, unless . . . as you say, in the commission. He probably surrounds himself with a lot of rare valuables. Be careful, Arthur.'

'Always.'

Dressing quickly, he called his sergeant from the downstairs phone and headed out, only stopping to pull on his overcoat and pet the cat. Hazel, familiar with these night excursions, executed the feline equivalent of a shrug and went back to sleep.

'Nice for some,' said St. Just.

DCI St. Just drove slowly, his sergeant at his side. The lighting around Hardwick College was medieval at best, with no moon to guide the way. Even though modern lanterns had replaced flickering torches on the main streets, the area around the college itself was gloomy. He turned on the car's high beams and light spilled over the cobblestones.

As directed by a young police constable, St. Just turned into a parking lot at the side of the college, an area marked off for official visitors and guests. He angled the car into a spot next to the coroner's unmarked vehicle. Judging by the already large police presence, he and Sergeant Fear were late to the party.

The car park had been built on a slight incline and the car

began rolling backwards. He set the handbrake and checked his watch. It was one in the morning.

St. Just and Fear made their way towards the commotion in Hardwick College's First Court. As they drew near, they could see a police cordon had already been established to keep the curious at bay. Gaggles of students wearing various combinations of pyjama bottoms and T-shirts had gathered round. The more foresightful had put on dressing gowns against the chill of the night air.

Flashing their identification, the two policemen joined a phalanx of technicians entering the scene, following them down a narrow hallway to what turned out to be the master's study at the back. Everyone there knew St. Just and stood back respectfully as they registered his presence.

He ignored them, as his attention was absorbed by the human body sprawled over the desk. A person somewhat elderly, going by the half of his face that was visible to him, but lean and fit-looking, dressed in a suit.

At first, he could see no indication of what had happened, but then a technician ignited the portable lights and the bloodstain on the man's back became apparent against the dark fabric of the suit jacket. The papers on his desk were askew – some were on the floor – and stained with spilt ink, to such an extent that St. Just thought the scene of literary chaos might have been staged. Whoever had killed him had been known to the victim, that much seemed clear, because normally people don't let anyone sneak up behind them unless there exists some level of trust.

Unless they were invited into the room and were meant to be there.

It was as if someone had stood behind the man, looking *with* him at something on his desk, and then, with the master distracted by whatever it was, had taken his life.

There was blood, to be sure, but not a spray of blood such as one might expect from a stabbing. A professional weapon may have been used, a stiletto or something similarly thin and deadly that wouldn't leave gaping wounds.

Or a simple letter opener, perhaps?

He turned to the pathologist, Dr Pomeroy, a young man

new to the job but already busy establishing a reputation as a clever, insightful, and reliable expert.

'You got here quickly,' said St. Just.

'I live nearby. Besides, I haven't been to bed yet.'

'Do we have a time of death?'

'The night porter, who called it in, found him at midnight. Or rather, just after. The porter . . .' he paused to check his notes, '. . . Oliver Staunton, thought he heard a cry, but he wasn't sure because it was rather simultaneous with the bells. Apparently, there's a midnight bell that tolls from the chapel. The idea being everyone should be inside the gates at that point with their lights out. After midnight, mercifully, they turn down the volume – it's a mechanized timer – so people can get some sleep. But when the porter thought more about it, he thought he also heard something *beneath* the sound of the bells and went to investigate. Like a cry of alarm. A human cry.'

'He suspected some kind of assault?'

'No, not really, he thought it was students mucking about. I gather that's rather a feature of his job, like running an infant school, keeping the young charges in line, and trying to enforce naptime.'

'With a wound like that would blood have sprayed on the perpetrator?'

'There's always blood spatter, even microscopic.'

'When can you give us more on time and cause?'

Pomeroy checked his watch. 'It'll probably be another twenty-four hours . . . tomorrow morning, first thing. I'll prepare a file for the coroner. No doubt of an inquest.'

That would be Fenwick, of course. The post of coroner dated back to the eleventh century, and Fenwick looked as if he might have been alive then. Any death as unnatural (let alone, as high profile) as this one would certainly trigger an inquest.

St. Just nodded his thanks, turning from Pomeroy to look around the room for signs of anything looking extra or out of place. The study was exactly as one might expect for a high-ranking Cambridge academic; anything modern seemed to have been carefully tucked away behind mahogany. The entire room was panelled wood and quite beautiful, burnished to a glow by centuries of polishing. An ormolu carriage clock on the mantelpiece ticked softly in the background.

The master must have had a personal computer, but it was nowhere in evidence, perhaps stashed inside the mahogany desk. Still, the paperwork scattered round indicated a pen-and-ink kind of guy. St. Just could relate. His own relationship with his computer at work was generally fraught with banked hostilities, but he had to admit he'd recently been impressed by AI's ability to identify crime hotspots in town. The force was seldom wasted these days in patrolling the wrong areas.

To his left were rows of wooden shelves bowing under the weight of heavy books – some antique and leather-bound, some modern. The bottom shelves were crowded with over-sized art books. These were the expensive kinds of volumes with colour plates that a man in the master's position would buy, the way that other people bought fresh bread.

He wondered a bit at that. How much of a master's time was spent on his field of expertise, and how much on the day-to-day running of what was in effect a small corporation such as Hardwick College? Or in giving lectures, for that matter?

To his right were more books on two floor-to-ceiling shelves, but between these shelves hung several paintings. He guessed they would be of some value, or hold a particular meaning for the master, or he would not have adorned his office with them. He couldn't guess at the artists' names. They were all quite small, all vaguely of the Rembrandt and Vermeer era to his untutored eye, and almost certainly originals.

Sergeant Fear returned to his side after chatting with the other policemen in the room.

'What do we have?' St. Just asked.

'Right now, just the bare bones of the situation. The station got a call from the college porter at twelve after midnight, stating that just after twelve o'clock he'd found a body in the Master's Lodge.'

'Why didn't he report it straightaway? He didn't have a mobile phone?'

'I gather not, sir. He went back to the Porters' Lodge and called it in on the landline there.'

'The master doesn't look to have suffered or struggled,' St. Just ventured. 'There would likely be more disturbance.'

'And what disturbance there is seems rather staged, if you don't mind my saying so, sir.'

'You thought so too? Yes, I find that interesting. There's been a clumsy attempt at cover-up, meaning a cover-up of the motive. Making it look like a burglary by someone unknown to the master. Although he would not have allowed a stranger at his back, would he?'

'Not unless it was someone who could move at the speed of light,' said Fear. 'The victim would have turned at least partially to ward off an attack.'

'What do we know about motive?' This last St. Just addressed to a passing constable he recognized from the local station. He remembered his unusual last name was Abelard.

'I've only been able to speak with the porter,' he replied. 'He mentioned something about paintings and artwork. But of course, what we do know is the master was an art expert of some kind. Don't ask me. I know what I like, and that's the extent of it. But we can assume he might have had something in his study worth stealing.'

St. Just stood back to survey the room, this time with an eye to finding a gaping hole in the array of paintings on the wall.

But everything there was neatly arranged in a pleasing aspect. Not necessarily lined up or stacked in order of size, but with a discerning appreciation for how to draw the eye from one object to another. Here and there, stacks of paintings were leaning against the wall or the bookcases, a few dozen in all. They didn't look disturbed. Of course, someone would have to go through and inventory them.

The cases themselves were too tightly packed with books to hold any sort of ornament. Nothing seemed to be missing there either.

What was a bit odd was the lack of personalization. The office clearly was the master's centre of business, but most people allowed for a photo or two of a loved one. There was nothing like that in this place of work. St. Just supposed that's how you got to the top of your profession. He wondered if the man had ever wondered if it was worth it.

For himself, he knew he was a bit of a workaholic, but meeting Portia had changed him in that regard. He was much more interested in spending his time with her now, as much as the job allowed.

Which was never quite enough.

'What do we know about his family or connections or enemies?' St. Just asked.

Abelard shook his head. His hair stood out from his skull at all angles. He looked as if he had been awakened from a deep sleep, but he had to have been on duty to have arrived at the scene before St. Just and Fear.

These fashion trends always baffled St. Just. His own hair was always neatly smoothed back against his head, as he believed it should be.

'We don't know yet,' said Abelard. 'Early days.'

'Get up on it and let us know. Send whatever you've got to Serious Crime.'

'Yes, sir.'

'We're going to need an accounting for his movements this evening. Anything from the porter on that?'

'The porter wasn't really all that coherent. Strange for an old army man, which he clearly is – most of these porters are. He must've seen a lot in his day, but . . .'

'But he thought he had reached a place of safety with this college gig,' St. Just finished for him. 'Nothing to do but keep the tourists out in term and shut down the occasional loud party.'

'Something like that, sir. I wonder if he's up to the job now it includes dealing with murder.'

'Well, how many of us really are?'

Sergeant Fear, having wandered off to take notes on the scene, which would include a rough sketch of the room and the position of the body, now walked up to St. Just, deliberately turning his back on the local policeman. Possibly a bit of rivalry there?

'There's a crowd forming outside. They're taking photos on their mobiles. Probably videos, too.'

'Move the cordon out a bit. We don't want anyone trampling in front of the lodge. And we really don't need close-ups of the scene on social media.'

Interviewing witnesses in the middle of the night was going to be a challenge, as there were potentially so many of them. At least they were all together in one spot for the moment.

'Get some people out to talk to the crowd, since they're there anyway, snapping photos of themselves.'

'Selfies,' provided Sergeant Fear helpfully.

'Right,' said St. Just. 'Have them ask if anyone is an eyewitness or if they're just rubbernecking. Any witnesses, obviously, we'll want to talk to, so get names and numbers. Also, let's see about CCTV.'

'On it,' said Fear. He gave Abelard a glance that clearly said his assistance wouldn't be welcome.

This was very unlike Fear. St. Just wondered if he'd had a run-in with the dishevelled policeman at some time in the past.

'Meanwhile, I'll go and speak with the porter,' said St. Just. 'I assume he's still in the Porters' Lodge?'

'In need of a drink, if you ask me,' said Abelard. At the virtuous smirk on his face, St. Just began to understand Fear's dislike.

'It's a good thing we didn't ask you,' said Sergeant Fear.

FIVE

Hear No Evil

'I'm not past it, if that's what you're thinking,' the night porter of Hardwick College insisted. 'I'd have seen anything amiss.'

'I didn't mean to imply you were past it, sir,' said St. Just. 'It's not necessarily a job for a young man. It's a job for someone with two good eyes, some common sense, and a lifetime of experience.' He was staring at the rather thick glasses the porter wore as he said this.

'The glasses are for close-up work,' said Oliver Staunton defensively. 'My distance vision is good, even at night, and that's what is needed for the night watch.'

'Of course,' said St. Just. 'I intended no insult.'

'Besides, with these cameras everywhere? No one's getting away with anything.'

'Security cameras have been a godsend for law enforcement, that's true. The sad fact is they are generally more useful for forensic analysis than for catching people red-handed.'

'True enough. Anyway, do you want to see what we've got on the cameras for the night?'

'Yes, I'd appreciate it.'

Oliver led him deeper inside the Porters' Lodge, where he had a homey little sitting room with a fireplace. It was comfortable, probably conducive to a nap in front of the telly, but there was a doorbell outside the lodge so if anyone needed the porter's attention, they only had to ring.

The problem being, of course, that burglars didn't tend to ring a bell and ask for admittance. No more than murderers did.

'As you can see,' said the porter, 'there are three screens, aimed at the three main courts.'

'Nothing aimed at, say, the car park area? I didn't notice any security there.'

The porter shrugged. 'I wasn't consulted about the installation. The powers that be didn't want the outer walls of the college to be marred with the things as well as the inner walls. Can't say I disagree. To be honest, I think it's more to mollify the parents. Make them feel someone's keeping an eye on things.'

'And the cameras rotate, it would appear,' said St. Just.

'Yes. They pan the area and then pan back. It's not foolproof, but you'd have to be moving fast to avoid detection when the camera doesn't happen to be pointing your way.'

'Not foolproof,' St. Just repeated, thinking: *And there is the rub.* The things were worse than useless. Anyone who spent even a moment studying the set-up would know to stand in the shadows, wait for the camera to be recording the opposite way, and then make a sprint for it.

It suggested to him that a young person might be involved, but any relatively fit man or woman could have done the same.

'Were the gates locked? I mean the outer gates into the college?'

The porter hesitated. 'I may have let that slide a bit. It hardly matters – midnight, or a quarter past midnight. No one comes and goes late at night, not even on a weekend. Besides, the cameras are there to catch every movement, more or less. Sometimes, like as not, it's an animal. We've had urban foxes lately – didn't use to. And anyway, I was wide awake.'

'Any particular reason?'

'Coffee.'

'But I'm sure you always drink coffee on a night shift.'

'I was expecting a call from my grandson. He doesn't call that often, so . . . He's got a young family now, and he said he would come to Cambridge with them sometime before Christmas. See me and visit his mother, too. She lives across town. I wouldn't miss that phone call.' He paused, adding, 'I wouldn't've fallen asleep.' But there was uncertainty in his voice.

'Did he call? It might be useful to be able to put a time stamp on events.'

But Oliver wouldn't meet St. Just's eye. The answer was obvious – no, he had let his grandfather down. St. Just didn't like distressing the man but murder cases had a way of doing that.

'I'm sure he'll call soon, sir. Young people have their own lives; they simply get busy and forget.'

'He's always been reliable.' This was not strictly true. Gerry had given his parents more than a moment's worry. 'It's just with the kids and all, you know . . .'

'Can you tell me what did happen before midnight? Anything out of the ordinary?'

'Lots of things. People think I just sit here all night like an old geezer, but in term the students keep me on my toes.'

'What kind of things, sir?'

'That American boy, Rufus Penn,' he said promptly. 'From Yale. He thinks I don't know he has a girlfriend come most nights to stay with him. She's the daughter of a woman attached to the college, and I would be amazed if Professor Beadle-Batsford approved. Anyway, all students are told to sign in any guests at the Porters' Lodge, but does Rufus bother with that? Not he. It's to comply with fire and safety regulations, not just on my say-so. If the place burned to the ground, we'd need to know who was here to rescue, you understand. Students may have a guest in their room for a maximum of nine nights per term, and the guest may not stay for longer than three nights consecutively. Those are the rules.'

'That's generous compared with, oh, say, the nineteenth century.'

'It's not forbidden altogether like it was back in the day, no, but in term it's not encouraged because the other students don't like it. The noise and carry-on, you know. They're trying to study.'

'Oh.'

'In my experience, some years ago now, mind, young love is not as interesting to other people as it is when it's happening to you. I wouldn't mind so much but it's my job to handle the complaints. And it's awkward, you understand.'

'Certainly, I understand. What else can you tell me about Rufus Penn? Where can I find him?'

'Third Court. Staircase C. Reading art history. Graduate degree. Home is upstate New York, whatever that means.'

'Art history, you say.'

'I could look up more on him if you like. I have the particulars on all the students, you know. Including emergency contact information.'

'Thank you. That may be useful later.' Given the master's field of expertise, surely a student of art history would have come to his attention?

'Did this Rufus Penn have any special access to the master, given his area of study?'

The porter shrugged and looked off into the distance. 'I don't know . . . I don't think so. It's early days. They all just got here.'

'Did anything else happen on your watch?'

'What time of the night are we talking about? I'm here from ten until six in the morning.'

I wish I knew, thought St. Just. Aloud he said, 'The autopsy will tell us more.'

'I thought I heard *something* at midnight. But the chapel bells go off then, and the sound got drowned out by that racket.'

'Those bells, are they accurate?'

'Oh, yes. Programmed to ring automatically, of course. We don't have a Quasimodo to ring the bells; it's all done on a timer these days. But that's what makes them accurate. Only time they aren't accurate is some sort of mechanical failure that is soon put right.'

'Someone tampering with the system? Is that possible?'

The porter shrugged. 'I suppose anything's possible. One of the kids reading engineering or the like might do it for a lark.'

'But you thought you could rely on CCTV, anyway? If something was amiss?'

'Yes, and normally I do. There was a palaver over getting that system installed but the porters can't be in ten places at once. Like I said, it's to keep the parents happy. When you're dealing with these old buildings, no one wants to stick some ugly old camera on the beautiful old stone, is all. There was a protest, lasted two days. Letters to the editor of the local paper, and so on . . . But pay that no mind. We must move with the times. I keep hearing from my grandson how I need to keep up with the times.'

'I don't see we are given much choice,' said St. Just.

The porter nodded. 'Not at any age. No.'

St. Just added, 'I must say, in my day, a locked outer gate didn't mean a lot.'

'I take your meaning, sir. I cannot account for the lax standards at other colleges.'

'Peterhouse is hardly known for its lax standards,' said St. Just, more sharply than he'd intended.

'Peterhouse? Why didn't you say so? I know the porter there. Ralph Standish. Ex-army, fine bloke. All right, yes, the more limber of the students will scale the walls, even when there's no need for it. As a lark, you know. To prove something to themselves. Mainly to impress a girl. The security cameras put a stop to most of that. No one can climb that fast.'

But, thought St. Just, the cameras are positioned *on* the rooftops, not aimed at the rooftops. There would be a way round those cameras. If it came to that, he'd call out a hearty young constable to test the possibilities. Maybe the one with the hair.

'How long had you known the master?' he asked Oliver.

'Since I had this job. Going on three year.'

'Did you know him well?'

'Wasn't my job to know him well. It was my job to keep a respectful distance and go about my business.'

'When did you see him last?'

'Before I saw him dead, you mean? That night, at ten. The master was just coming in as I was taking up my post – taking over from Aled Evans. Evans covers the afternoons and evenings.'

'Did you speak to him, the master?'

'Just to say hello. In passing, you know.'

'You're quite certain it was the master.'

'Course I'm certain. I'm not blind, you know.'

'How did he seem? Anything out of the ordinary?'

The porter shook his head. 'Same as always.'

'In a hurry? Distracted? Happy? Inebriated?'

'Same as always,' Oliver repeated. 'And he didn't drink. Not like you're saying.'

'And before that? Did he go out for dinner and stay out till ten?'

'I guess he was out at dinner. He sometimes dined at other colleges.'

'At what time did he leave for dinner?'

'I don't know. You'll have to ask Evans. It's his shift. Two in the afternoon until I come on at ten. Seven days a week in term. It's a hard schedule, it is, but out of term we get a break. No one around but tourists then. And they're easy. All agog, you know. All "look at the turrets".'

'Very well, we will have to get a statement from Evans. If you'll provide us with his contact information?'

'Certainly I will do that, but I can save you some time.'

'Oh?'

'I called both of the other porters already. I knew it would be important, you see. And they'd both need to know what they'd be walking into today. Evans said the master went out for dinner, but he wasn't sure where or what time.'

'He specifically said dinner?'

'I'm not sure. It was dinnertime, maybe that's what he meant.'

The police would need a word with Evans, although knowing what time the master left for dinner wasn't critical. Like most cases, this one would have ever-shifting priorities, so it would be a matter of fitting Evans in.

'I suppose the master of the college wasn't required to sign out.'

'No, indeed. The very idea. No, he's free to come and go; it's not our business to question the master's whereabouts. Evans did sign in a man to see him yesterday afternoon. That would be before he left for dinner or wherever he was going. A man named Ambrose something. Knickknack, something like that. He signed the logbook if you'd like to see it.'

'Indeed, I would.'

The porter hauled himself to his feet, went into the outfacing porters' office, and came back carrying a heavy leather-bound visitors' book open to the most recent entries.

'See right there.' He pointed.

St. Just looked at the page. Written in a neat hand, he saw:

Name: Ambrose Nussknacker

Time of visit: 5 p.m.

Purpose of visit: Sir Flyte

In a different hand was the notation that Ambrose Nussknacker had taken his leave of the college at 5.58 p.m. The precision of that time made him wonder if Ambrose had rounded the time of his arrival to the nearest number and Evans, being more precise, had noted the actual time of his departure, but St. Just didn't feel that it mattered. Oliver Staunton had told him he'd seen the master alive and well at ten that night when he took up his shift. Supposedly the porter Evans, just heading off his shift, could confirm that sighting.

'Did Evans say he'd seen the master come back in at ten?'

'He was in the back room here, getting ready to leave and shouting out something to me about the schedule for next week, so he didn't see him, no.'

Oh, well. Did it matter? It didn't get them much further forward, except a visit to this Ambrose Nussknacker might be worthwhile, to learn more about the master's state of mind in the hours leading up to his death. They'd also need to find out where Sir Flyte had been that evening. Presumably he'd have taken a car if he were going any great distance.

'Did the master drive a car?'

'An old Audi, yes.'

St. Just would have someone verify that his car was where he normally left it, but if the master had been seen walking out of the college's main gate, it meant he left his car in the car park beside the college, the area he and Fear had parked in that morning. Had an Audi been there? He couldn't be sure in the dark and commotion.

'Did Evans see the master get into a car or a taxi?'

'He said the master was walking up King's Parade last he saw the back of him. Oh, that was badly put, I mean . . .'

'Evans saw him walking away.'

'That is correct. Towards the town proper, headed up King's Parade.'

'I see. Now, it would be immensely helpful if I knew a bit

of the master's background and character from someone who, after all, must've had some dealings with him, coming and going day by day.'

'I saw less of him than the other porters, you know. It was rare to see him at ten at night or after, and rarer still to see him at six in the morning. I mostly know what I know about his usual movements second hand, and that from Aled Evans and Zola Blaze, the other porters. The master had been at the college since he'd been a student, and as he'd been promoted through the ranks to lecturer and professor, he'd moved into better and better accommodation, ending up in the Master's Lodge. He'd been what they call a rising star from the first. People liked him. If they didn't like him or were jealous, which I think is more likely, they at least respected him.'

'But not enough apparently, Mr Staunton. *Were* there jealousies?'

'This is Cambridge. Of course there were jealousies. Who wrote this, who got credit for that, who published more papers, who invented what first. These dons can be like a bunch of hens trying to peck each other to death. Even I knew he was famous, so jealousy went with the territory.'

'Do you really think someone would murder him for being more famous than they were?'

'Sure. I've seen all sorts in my day. Men killing in wartime, now – that's a different story. You do what's needed to be done. No hard feelings, so to speak. Something cold-blooded like this, in civilized Cambridge? Hard to see it, but anything's possible.'

'We in the police see it every day, actually,' St. Just murmured.

'I would've said the master never harmed anyone – at least not deliberately. He wasn't a fighter. He was a thinker. Know what I mean? If they killed him, and it looks like they did, it was for some crazy reason of their own. Maybe because *they* wanted to be on top as he'd always been. Me, I'm sorry he's gone. Not least because the rest of them will start kicking off the moment they think it's decent to do so, if not before.'

'What do you mean?'

'A vacuum has been created by the master's passing, and

you know what they say about nature and vacuums. Someone will be after the master's job and for a long while we won't know who to trust around here. They'll all be nice as pie to each other, but when backs are turned, well . . .'

'Do you mean there will be a bit of backstabbing?'

The porter stared at him from behind those thick lenses.

'That was thoughtless,' said St. Just. 'I meant to say, there will be some bad-mouthing?'

'I'm afraid so, sir. It'll be nonstop. And even after someone's elected, grudges will be held and cherished. This lot remembers a slight from centuries past. It's in their natures.'

I hope we won't have to go back centuries to solve this, thought St. Just.

Aloud he said, 'Thank you for your time. No, don't get up.' He could tell Oliver Staunton had a problem with his knees and standing was painful, let alone walking or running. He certainly was not built for chasing down suspects or students.

Even if he could see or hear them clearly.

'I'll see myself out.'

SIX

Rufus Penn

While he was on the grounds of Hardwick College, St. Just thought he'd see if he could find the American, Rufus Penn, in his rooms in Staircase C. A night owl such as the porter described may have seen or heard something relevant to the case.

First, he went to collect Sergeant Fear from the crime scene. He didn't want to have to rely on memory for another interview. He paused just outside the Porters' Lodge by the main college gate to jot down the highlights from his conversation with Oliver Staunton. There would seem to be little question, taking the porter at his word, that the master had returned to the college at ten, coinciding with the porters' shift change.

And after that?

What happened after that was what he and Fear needed to discover.

They found Rufus Penn in his rooms in the college's Third Court. The rooms were a colossal tip, even by the standards of young people away from home and on their own, some for the first time. Papers and computers and clothing and sports equipment and large art books were flung haphazardly around the narrow bed and on the built-in shelves. It was a miracle Rufus could make his way to the bed or find a spot on it to sleep.

St. Just wondered idly what the college bedder made of it. There was no way anyone could keep any of this clean and dusted.

'And why are there questions from the police about this?' Rufus Penn asked, in reply to St. Just's first routine question as to his whereabouts the night before. 'I thought the master died of a heart attack or maybe a stroke. I mean, he was old, wasn't he?'

'Not as old as all that,' said St. Just.

'It's just nature's way, isn't it?' said Rufus. 'Making way for the new. If you've run out of things to do, my bicycle was stolen the other day. Happens all the time around here, the police said when I phoned to report it. It's why I thought you were here talking to me.'

'Yes, Serious Crime routinely chases up bicycle thieves.'

Rufus paused, then: 'You're being sarcastic, aren't you? It's hard to tell with you Brits. I thought you were supposed to be polite.'

'We are, sir, situationally. But as far as we know that's the case – that the master's heart gave out. But we don't know much more yet.'

That wasn't anywhere near the truth, of course. He'd just been on the mobile with the coroner who was certain the full run of tests would conclude what was evident, that death had been caused by massive bleeding from stab wounds to the heart and lungs. But until it was official, St. Just thought it best to throttle the rumour mill while there was still time. Panic was inevitably coming, within and without the gates of Hardwick College, but he wanted to control it as much as he could while people were calm and could gather their memories in a peaceful state of mind.

He looked hard at Rufus, who had yet to endear himself. He had a fresh-faced, boyish charm to go with a well-defined jawline, expressive eyes, and the sort of bright smile Americans seem to be issued at birth. He wore black jeans, a T-shirt featuring the college's coat of arms, and expensive trainers. He was clean-cut, no beard, short hair. The slightly too small T-shirt emphasized his athletic build. St. Just felt himself trying to hold in his stomach but quickly gave up the effort. There was much to be said for easing into a comfortable middle age.

'So, what brings you to Cambridge?' St. Just asked.

'I wouldn't think that required an answer,' said Rufus Penn.

'Would you mind answering, anyway?' From the corner of his eye, he saw Sergeant Fear's lifted brow as he took notes. The interview was not off to a good start if snark was going to be the baseline.

'It's always just been *there*, you know?' Penn replied. 'A

dream, a goal. My family is into art, always has been. My father taught art at Georgetown – I mean, the history of art. We're all big Anglophiles, and Cambridge is part of our tradition.'

'Most flattering.'

Rufus added: 'My grandfather came here – although the war interrupted his studies, they needed his expertise – as did my father. The British girls are bright and pretty and they like my accent. Does that answer your question?'

'I understand you're from upstate New York. Where exactly?'

'Albany. But I grew up in Washington, DC.'

Now they were getting somewhere. Rufus was volunteering information.

'Your father was from Washington, DC?'

'No.'

With exaggerated patience, St. Just asked, 'Where. Was. Your. Father. From? Sir.'

'He was from Albany. No one in DC is from DC. They all come there for the job and then leave as soon as possible. Have you ever been to the British Embassy?'

'No.'

'I dated a daughter of the ambassador at the time. Awesome.'

It wasn't clear if he meant the daughter or the embassy, but at least he was talking.

This line of questioning seemed to have nothing to do with what had happened to the master, but St. Just wasn't inclined to let Rufus off easily. For one thing, he found the young man's hyper-confidence grating. Rufus was operating above his age in that department. St. Just supposed that was good reason to commend both him and his upbringing.

But some part of St. Just, some little part he didn't care to examine too closely, wanted to find the soft spot. Everyone had one.

He was there with Fear mainly because of a chance remark by the porter explaining why he'd gone to investigate in the first place. That and his assumption that Rufus would be at the heart of any disturbance in the courts. It was hardly a strong tie to the case, but so long as they were in the area . . .

'So. Again. Can you tell us your movements of last night?'

'I went out to dinner at someone's house. This girl I've been seeing, her mother invited me. She's head of women's studies at the university – the mother, I mean. Peyton doesn't really do anything.'

'So it was just the three of you?'

'There was the curator of a local museum. Ambrose Nussknacker.'

'You don't say?'

'I do. Why? Is it important?'

St. Just wasn't sure. But the master had been an art history expert and, suddenly, the world of art history was beating down St. Just's door.

'The master didn't join you?'

'No. Why should he?'

'You and Ambrose must have had a great deal to talk about.'

'Well, it's a funny thing,' said Rufus, suddenly cautious. 'He did mention he had been talking with the master recently about methods of evaluating art. The newest methods, I mean. Artificial Intelligence. The master was strongly opposed to its use, I gather.'

'How recently?'

'Nussknacker didn't say. Just, recently.'

'How strongly?'

'He just said strongly. I don't know, do I?'

'I see. What time did you return to your rooms from dinner?'

'Late. I went back out, you see. Nussknacker dropped me off back at the college, but I decided the night was still young and I wanted a nightcap.'

'What time, again?'

'If you must know—'

'Take that as given. We're the police.'

'All right, keep your shirt on. The dinner party started at eight. It ended about quarter to eleven. Ambrose dropped me back at the college about eleven. I went out for a drink and returned after midnight to this commotion around the Master's Lodge.'

St. Just sighed. The business of checking and verifying alibis would be never-ending. They'd have to speak with the curator, Nussknacker.

'Where did you go for your nightcap?'

Rufus named a pub popular with students. Of course, they'd have to check – St. Just had learned alibis are too often built of straw to be set aflame later in court – but it seemed Rufus was well-alibied for the crime.

Sergeant Fear spoke up, surprisingly. Fear usually stayed out of interviews, seeing his roles as observer and documenter.

'What do you plan to do in the future?' Fear asked Rufus Penn.

After a pause bordering on rudeness, Penn replied, 'If it's relevant, I plan to teach.'

'Back at Harvard?'

'It's Yale, actually.' There was the merest suggestion of a snarl as he delivered this reply.

And there it was. They'd found the soft spot: the fragile ego beneath the carapace. The rivalry between the two established seats of learning in the United States was legendary, only to be matched by that between Oxford and Cambridge.

'Oh,' said Sergeant Fear innocently, 'I understood Harvard had the more prestigious department for art history studies, but I could be wrong.'

'I don't think a cop would really know anything about it,' said Penn. 'And it happens not to be true. Now, if there's nothing else . . .'

'We do have some standard questions,' said St. Just. 'We're looking for witnesses, people who might have seen what went on in the hours surrounding the time the master met his end.'

'I just told you I wasn't here.'

'Just for clarity,' St. Just said smoothly. 'So we can eliminate you from our inquiries.'

'For example?' The young man looked at his watch. It was a hint for them to leave and he was none too subtle about it. It was one of those watches designed to calibrate the number of steps taken each day, the rate of the wearer's heartbeat, and so forth. As the policemen watched, Penn pressed a couple of little buttons on the thing.

What was he doing – setting a timer for the interview? The gesture irritated St. Just to no end.

'Are you late for something, Mr Penn?'

'I will be.'

'Just a few questions,' he repeated. 'We'll be talking to everyone in your stairwell and in the court. To establish a timeline, you know.'

This was a bit of an exaggeration, although as St. Just said the words, he realized what a massive task lay ahead of them just to set the basics of an investigation. The police had put out a notice via the college's internal email list asking anyone with any information to come forward. He fully expected to see the usual contingent of helpful witnesses, mixed with hopeful witnesses.

Some would be more useful than others, but they all had to be interviewed. There was something about being in the vicinity of a murder that made honest citizens want to be part of the action, even if they had to invent their role. They would have heard someone running or people quarrelling or the sound of gunshots – they were sure of it. Or the sound of running water after midnight – and they'd never heard that before. Or a meteor appearing over the Master's Lodge, just in time to illuminate a dark, skulking figure.

Nothing they said could be dismissed outright but eventually, most of it would be.

Then would come the usual clamour from the local news that the murder of the master of a college was getting more attention than the murder of a drug addict on the streets of Cambridge. He supposed Barnard LaFarge, the *Bugle*'s main if not its only reporter, would be leading the charge.

This was to some degree true and there was nothing to be done about it. But it was a skewed perception that the Cambridge police didn't care about the death on the streets of a beggar or drug addict. The murder of a renowned scholar and pillar of the tightly knit academic community was something that would resonate with the people of the city – with everyone, town and gown – and do immediate and lasting damage.

Suddenly they would feel unsafe. Most of them knew better than to be out on the dodgier streets of Cambridge on a dark night, sober or intoxicated. At midnight, most of them expected to be safe in their homes or college rooms, tucked up in their soft beds.

The master had been murdered not just in his home, but in his vastly historic and famous home. Hardwick College had produced some of the world's greatest minds down through the centuries – the prime ministers, the heads of businesses, the writers and actors, the famous scientists who'd made world-changing discoveries and inventions.

Furthermore, there would be the usual salacious speculation over what the man might have been doing to provoke such an attack. People felt there had to be a *reason*. Otherwise, no one was safe.

It was up to St. Just and Sergeant Fear and whoever they could corral into the investigation to find out the reason. Otherwise, they were looking at a random attack, and if so, God help them. Every person on the street knew one random attack could lead to a dozen more. What Cambridge did not need was its own Jack the Ripper.

As it was, he knew he'd be hearing from every head of every college – all thirty-one of them – before the day was out, asking for protection the police would be too understaffed to provide.

SEVEN
The Curator

Ambrose Nussknacker was what the French would have called *jolie laide* had he been a woman. Interesting features, unconventionally arranged, but fascinating when taken as a whole. Bushy dark eyebrows, frosty white hair. A man who might have been drawn to beautiful objects because he himself had just missed being what the world might consider beautiful.

Beauty being always in the eye of the beholder.

Age had added a few pounds and a few chins, but this did not detract from the man's appeal. His demeanour was courtly but relaxed, that of a person accustomed to the company of the upper classes and good at convincing them that donating their family treasures to his bijou gallery and museum would be a good idea. He probably specialized in dealing with elderly people with dwindling friends and families, worried that the treasures they left behind wouldn't be properly treasured.

After a few minutes in his company, St. Just also sensed a solid businessman behind the bonhomie.

They had arranged an early meeting at the café inside St Michael's Church on Trinity Street. Ostensibly, St. Just wanted Ambrose Nussknacker to weigh in on how to establish the authenticity of a painting – assuming artwork might have something to do with the master's demise.

Not ostensibly, Nussknacker was a subject in a murder investigation, being a person known to have been with the master in his study not long before he was killed in that study.

At the least, he would have seen the study before it was disturbed – artfully rearranged, in St. Just's and Fear's opinion – by the murderer.

So far, no one had been able to establish where the master had been during the hours between six and ten when he returned to his college the night he was killed. His whereabouts were likely significant and St. Just had people working on it via the magic of CCTV.

The problem was they didn't know if – once out of the porter's sight – the master had been driven off somewhere in a taxi or a car, if he'd circled back and taken his own car, or if he'd walked somewhere. The anti-terror barriers on King's Parade limited automobile traffic during the day, which would marginally aid the search. There was nothing to stop pedestrians or bicycles, however.

In the meantime, while camera footage was being studied for clues, Ambrose Nussknacker would have to do.

Over coffee and a chocolate croissant, St. Just asked him if the master had discussed any of his plans when he'd seen him – particularly his plans for the evening before he died. Steam from the coffee warmed the air between them, the smell helping revive St. Just, who was operating on a very few hours of sleep.

Ambrose shook his head. 'No. I don't think he went out much in the evenings except on occasion to dinners at other colleges. And he wasn't wearing his gown, as he would do for sitting at High Table. That's not to say he couldn't have put it on after I left.'

'He was wearing a suit when he was with you, was he?'

'Quite a nice suit, yes. Old, but timeless. He had impeccable taste and kept his clothing altered to suit the times.'

'I see.' The same suit he'd been wearing when he was murdered, it sounded like.

'His office was in good order, was it? Nothing out of place that you could see?'

'Same as always. He was an organized individual.'

'I wanted to talk to you partly because of your expertise, an expertise you shared with the master.'

'He was an academic, so in a way his knowledge was superior to mine. At least – to some extent. I've been at this a long time.'

'But you might know more about the business side. By that I mean, the art valuation business.'

'Well, yes, and nowadays there are many more methods than

before to know about,' Nussknacker said. 'Infrared reflectography, scanning electron microscopy, cross-section evaluation. We no longer have to rely on anyone's say-so, no matter how expert they may be. The master seemed to think, with Cambridge spy Anthony Blunt, that connoisseurship was what counted, not data.'

'I always thought establishing provenance – where the painting came from, how it was handed down from where to where – was key.'

'Yes, that's a big part of it, of course. But you would be amazed at what goes on. It's as easy to forge a sales receipt as it is to forge a painting. What am I saying? It's easier to forge a sales receipt. You simply need the right sort of paper and ink from the right period of history, a paper carrying a logo and a signature that looks like what is known to be authentic. Beyond that . . .'

'Yes?'

'Well, the truth is people see what they want to believe they're seeing. Especially in the art world, which is not noted for sanity in this regard. Any collector or curator who covets a great painting will overlook the glaring clues to the fact that it is a forgery. I have felt the urge myself, many a time. Someone rang me one day claiming to have what they swore was a page torn from the First Folio of Shakespeare. From *King Lear*, I think it was. Oh, I so much wanted it to be true. But when the man showed up in my office with it, immediately I could tell. The man was a nutter and the paper was from a high-street stationer. It was all but typewritten.'

'That should have made your job easy.'

He smiled. It was a disarmingly lopsided smile. 'I've had more people than I can count come to me with some offering from their great-aunt Mary's attic. It's a regular *Antiques Roadshow* in my office. Often the article is authentic but worthless, nonetheless. And no one wants to hear that verdict.'

St. Just paused for a sip of coffee. 'I understand you and the master had, shall we say, a difference of opinion over the use of AI in determining the value of paintings.'

'We didn't come to blows, if that's what you're implying.'

'Not at all,' St. Just murmured dishonestly.

'Who on earth told you that? Oh, that American kid, I suppose. Rufus. If I'd known it would come to your attention, I would have been more discreet.'

Murder is like that, thought St. Just. By the end, no secrets are hidden.

'But I don't row with people. Especially in my line of work, I can't afford to. You must remain friendly. Not make friends, perhaps, but be friendly. The master, who often acted as an art advisor, also knew this. How to keep a friendly distance.'

'A bit like being the police.'

'Rufus could take a lesson in discretion,' Ambrose went on, still affronted by the accusation. 'He and I had a conversation after a dinner party we were both invited to. You don't bad-mouth your hostess – or rather, her daughter – while you're standing in their garden. Very bad form. Anyway, I take it his was not a natural death.'

'We are looking into it,' said St. Just vaguely. 'But this is a discussion you had with the master?'

Nussknacker also answered obliquely.

'You must know yourself, Inspector. AI is already useful in police investigations, just to name one area, and it's going to become more so. It's already disrupting the art world. Paintings that were sworn to be authentic are being revealed as either entirely fraudulent or, more often, as being the work of an apprentice to a great painter. Anyway, as a policeman I would think you would be dancing for joy. All the slog of finding criminals, sorting through old records – the time cut in half. Or more.'

What was it, St. Just wondered, people imagined he did all day. Sit at a computer languidly scrolling through databases to find criminals at their home addresses? Besides, the Cambridgeshire Constabulary had an entire team of people assigned to those sorts of tasks, trolling through vast amounts of data and evidence.

He would grudgingly admit their work might be sped up with AI finding patterns and connections but there was no substitute for a face-to-face interview.

Like this one.

St. Just sensed that despite his apparent affability there was something the man was holding back.

Show me a computer that can look into a man's eyes and tell me that.

'We have the pesky problem of invasion of privacy to get past first,' he said.

Nussknacker laughed briefly. 'At least we don't have that problem with the Old Masters. It's a regular Dead Artist's Society. They seldom complain.'

'And how often is AI wrong when it's applied to the collectible art world, anyway?'

'Not often. You'd be amazed.'

'It's said to be riddled with mistakes.'

'Fewer and fewer with each passing day. Ten years from now, I can see it replacing me as an expert, which is very good timing on the part of the universe because I plan on retiring just about then.'

'And what do you plan to do?'

'Why, I suppose I'll write a book. Ever since I was a student here, I've wanted to.'

St. Just thought him optimistic to imagine book writing wouldn't be replaced by a computer also but he said nothing.

'It's funny you should ask, but that's what the master and I talked mostly about the week before he died. AI.'

'The week before, you say?'

'Yes. I was a frequent visitor. I think it was about a week before. He had this painting he'd inherited, you see. Several of them, in fact. I did try to persuade him to let me have at least one of them evaluated using some of the modern techniques. He was having none of it.'

St. Just remembered where else he'd recently come across Nussknacker's name. There had been an article about the discovery of a possible Rembrandt a few days ago, and Nussknacker had been invoked as the expert to weigh in on its likely authenticity.

'You don't actually think he'd inherited a Rembrandt, do you?'

'I think we don't know. He wouldn't let me help him with it. Honestly, he was acting very strangely. I don't suppose you or your men . . .?'

'Came across a Rembrandt painting hanging in the Master's

Lodge? Not that I'm aware.' This was nothing but the truth – so far as St. Just knew. There had been paintings galore, but none that jumped out as an incalculably valuable Old Master painting. 'But if we do, you'll be the first to know. We'd need your expertise to help us evaluate it.'

'It would be my pleasure, entirely.' He dug a business card out of his pocket and handed it across the table. 'Please.'

St. Just refused the man's insistence on paying for his coffee and the croissant, and bade him farewell.

It was an ineffective bribe if that was what it was meant to be. St. Just would be keeping the amiable Ambrose Nussknacker high on his list of suspects.

They left Michaelhouse Café together and St. Just stood watching as Nussknacker pedalled his way down Trinity Street.

EIGHT
All the News

St. Just made a quick stop at HQ to check in with his team before meeting the *Bugle* reporter one and a half hours later.

Barnard LaFarge was about forty years old. He was grey-eyed with greying hair tousled and spiked at what must have been great trouble and expense. Given salaries for news people these days, St. Just thought it might have cost his entire pay packet for a week.

He wore jeans torn at the knees, a style perhaps more suited to a younger man, topped with a blue blazer over a pinstripe shirt unbuttoned at the collar. He seemed to run on a rather manic mainframe energy, practically vibrating as he took in his surroundings at yet another coffee shop, this time the Dark Brew in Bene't Street, eyes swivelling about the room, taking in everyone and everything. He might have made a good spy, albeit a not-too-subtle one.

St. Just would have sworn Barnard LaFarge wasn't paying attention, but throughout the conversation he would surprise him by parroting back what he'd said, almost word for word.

'You don't take notes?' St. Just asked him.

'No need.' LaFarge tapped the side of his head. 'Mind like a steel trap.'

'That must come in handy for a reporter.'

'It does. If there's a drawback to it, it's that I seldom have a written record of conversations.'

'So, if anyone ever challenges what happened, what was said . . .'

'It's never really happened. The challenge, I mean. The *Bugle* is a vanishingly small operation, to say the least, and besides, we pride ourselves on honest reporting. Much good does it do us.'

'I have my sergeant to rely on,' said St. Just. 'He seldom misses a word although he does editorialize a bit with witness statements.'

Barnard smiled. 'It makes me wish I had my own sergeant, that does. So, you had questions about my article on paintings? The piece where I quoted Ambrose Nussknacker?'

'Yes, it was quite well done.' Thanks to Portia, St. Just was aware how susceptible writers are to flattery. 'Engrossing. I might start by asking if you have a background in art history.'

'Working for a small newspaper I have a background in everything. Master of none, of course.'

'What is your background?'

'Academically my background is in English literature. It came highly recommended as a lucrative occupation.' He grinned to make sure St. Just heard the joke behind his words. 'But in truth, the only thing I do at all well is write, an ability a couple of my teachers noticed and encouraged. I could have gone into the law and written torts or whatever it is they do and made piles of money, I suppose, but it didn't interest me.'

'You are perhaps thinking of writing a novel?'

'I am writing a crime novel, as a matter of fact. Erm . . . I happen to know your wife is a well-known crime novelist. I don't suppose you might—'

'Perhaps. Now, please tell me about your conversation with Ambrose Nussknacker.'

'Well, it was a bit odd,' said LaFarge. 'He was dropping hints about a potential masterpiece that had been unearthed by one of the college masters who happened to be an expert in art history. He named no names, but I knew from various other things he said it almost had to be the master of Hardwick College. I wrote the story so other people could draw that conclusion as well. I hope that didn't cause any trouble for Sir Flyte. I did hear, of course, that he's dead.'

'I understand he had got hold of something that might be a Rembrandt.'

'Yes, and wouldn't that be something if it were true? Tell me, is it? All I saw were photographs. Most of it looked like rubbish to me, but it's not my field, so—'

'You saw what?'

'Photographs. Nussknacker had photos. Nothing professional – snapshots, really – taken with his mobile. A bit blurry. Nothing, I daresay, that could be used by an art expert to establish authenticity. He only showed them to me to bolster what he was talking about. He refused to let me have copies. And from that, I gathered, he may not have had any business having the photos in his possession.'

'I see.' Nussknacker had kept that to himself when St. Just had interviewed him earlier. Small wonder.

'But remember, I have a near-photographic memory. I can tell you most of what I saw of the paintings that day.'

'Which was?'

'A couple of lopsided-looking old people, two landscapes, a white horse standing in a field, a group picnic scene – that one looked to me like that famous Impressionist painting, the one with the nude. The white horse was more of a taupe horse and a lame one, at that. The pictures looked quite dirty, covered in this murky yellowing varnish, making them very hard to see. I don't wonder there was a question about them in the master's mind.'

'What else did you see?'

'Just one more painting. The best of them, I thought. A small portrait of a young woman wearing the usual Rembrandt kind of stuff.'

'How small?'

'At a guess, about the size of an A4 sheet of paper. Maybe a bit larger. There was nothing to indicate scale.'

'Could you expand on what you mean by "Rembrandt kind of stuff"?'

'A lace collar round her neck, lace at her wrists, and pearls. Jewels. A sort of costume studded with jewels.' St. Just nodded for him to go on. He was himself taking notes in the absence of Fear. 'Some kind of dark dress. She had a long face – she was rather homely, if I'm honest, but her colouring was pretty and she looked rather bold, if you know what I mean. Sure of herself. You could tell even through the grime she had these pink cheeks and dark eyes.'

'You do have a remarkable memory,' said St. Just.

'Oh, my memory is good. I just have trouble translating what I see into words at times.'

'I think you did rather well just now. Thank you. What kind of age would you say she was?'

'I don't know. Anything from a teenager to a woman of thirty-plus. With that rosy complexion, it's difficult to say and again, with the coat of varnish, it was hard to see the details. And I think kids in those days were dressed as adults from an early age, weren't they?'

'No jeans and T-shirts.'

'Correct. Oh, and she had an ornament in her hair, but that was impossible to see clearly. Why do people do that to valuable artwork? Smear it with varnish?'

'I don't know. I think these things go in phases but I'm sure the idea was to prevent the colours from changing and to give the whole thing a glossy finish. They never realized they were just adding to the problem of darkening the colours over time. You say the master had questions about the veracity or the value of these paintings?'

'Again, I'm just going by what I was told, but yes. He couldn't even be bothered to have them evaluated.'

'I would take that to mean they were of no value.'

'No, that's not exactly what Ambrose conveyed to me. The master was adamant about it, and really there was no reason. The techniques for evaluating a painting are straightforward – perhaps I could say much more straightforward – than in his day. And the cost wouldn't be as prohibitive as it once might have been. I've been reading up on the subject – fascinating stuff.

'But the first step likely would be to use artificial intelligence to scan a proper image, and the master absolutely would not go there. It was very strange behaviour. I mean, what harm would it do? It wouldn't damage the painting in any way. But someone would first need to take a proper photograph.'

'So again, the photos you saw were not what you would call proper photographs for professional evaluation.'

'Not at all. Some were of a few paintings lined up in a row so they could fit in one shot. Taken in a hurry, maybe. Again, if I'm honest, I don't think the master knew that Ambrose had taken the photos.'

'It's hard to imagine the master leaving him alone with these treasures, if they were treasures.'

'I suppose that strengthens the theory they were worthless, that the master wandered off to do something or was urgently called away and left Ambrose alone there with his mobile phone. But the master may not have thought in terms of phone cameras. He was not remotely a tech kind of guy, given what Ambrose told me. The very thought of AI terrifies a lot of sensible people, but they do tend to be people who are not conversant with the new technology, and just don't understand what it can do, the good it can do in medicine, climate change – the list goes on.'

'I suppose you would have to include me in that assessment. I'm a bit on the low-tech side, but I do understand the usefulness once it's shown to me. The value in police work has been remarkable.'

'I can imagine. Using it to scan CCTV footage alone would save hours. Anyway, from my point of view, it's a shame. I was already planning an article about how the paintings were going to be authenticated, working in some relevant information for the gadget-happy crowd. But the story just ended before it started, really. Without a good close-up shot of any of the paintings, let alone the one painting I thought was attractive, it was the end of the story.'

'I do see.'

'And with the master refusing to go any further, I couldn't turn it into one of those stories where everyone starts regretting that painting of Aunt Betty's they let go at a car boot sale for pennies, thinking now that maybe it was worth a fortune. The fact is that seldom happens. What looks like someone's rubbish is, most times, someone's rubbish.'

St. Just didn't see that the reporter knew much more than he had told him. It was hard to believe he had any connection to the case – unless he had recognized the value of one of the paintings immediately and raced over to kill the master and grab the one painting, the one potential Rembrandt, he thought was worthwhile. Or grab the lot, if only to cover his interest in the one painting.

But he was reminded it was time to verify with his team that all the paintings, the horse and nude and so on, were still in the master's study.

On the off chance, he asked the reporter, 'Where were you last night when the master was killed?'

'You mean all night?' LaFarge asked.

'Yes.' The police weren't releasing anything specific to the public just yet in case it gave people advance warning to line up their alibis as needed. St. Just certainly didn't want too much information about the murder getting into the paper. That, he was sure, was the only reason the reporter was so eager to talk to him – he was looking for an inside track on what had happened to the master.

That, and a possible introduction to Portia, with the hope of getting her assistance with his novel.

'I am sorry to disappoint you,' said LaFarge. 'And no offence taken that you ask – I realize you must. If I had had an eye on the main chance, I would've rushed over and stolen the paintings, or at least that one.'

'Did you?'

He smiled. 'That was meant as a joke, of course. I must emphasize that what I saw wasn't clear enough, good enough, or big enough to show me anything that would've spurred me on to kill a man over it, even if I were so inclined. But then, you've only my word for that.'

'So you won't mind telling me where you were?'

'Not at all. I was visiting my mother in a care home in Norfolk. It's about sixty miles each way. I go up there and stay the night in an inn so I can spend at least two hours with her. I can tell you the name of the place; they're quite used to my being there. I was there all night. And yes, I suppose I could've driven back to kill the master and grab the paintings, but I did not. You'll have to take my word for it.'

Somehow, St. Just did.

'One final question. What was Nussknacker after, in showing you the photos? Did he say what his angle was?'

'Only indirectly. If you want my best guess, he was hoping to force the master's hand. To raise enough interest in the art world and beyond that there would have to be a proper evaluation done. I mean, a newly discovered Rembrandt? The master couldn't keep that to himself.'

And more to the point, why would he want to? thought St. Just. It simply didn't add up.

'Thank you, sir, for your time.'

He handed St. Just his card. 'Anytime.'

NINE
Dinner with Portia

'So, tell me all about it,' said Portia as he sat down at the dinner table at their new home in Hemingford Abbots. They'd chosen the village for its beauty and convenience, being about twenty minutes from her job in Cambridge and ten from his HQ in Huntingdon.

She placed before him a bowl of beef bourguignon, a basket of freshly baked bread, and a plate of butter, then poured a glass of wine for them both.

'You're not eating?'

'Already have.'

He glanced at his watch.

'Oh, God. I'm sorry.'

'No need to apologize. Just tell me what you've been up to today.'

'You probably know as much as I do if you've been reading the papers.'

'Yes, I have,' she said. 'Online. Every word. There's one reporter who seems to have made it his case. Even riddled with pop-up ads, it's a compelling story.'

'That would be Barnard LaFarge,' said St. Just.

'That's it. This will probably be a career maker for him. He'll be off to London soon. The bright lights. In a former time, I might have said he's headed for Fleet Street, but by and large there is no Fleet Street anymore. London got too expensive.'

'I spoke with him today.'

'Not as a suspect?'

'Early days. The beef is delicious, by the way. And the pearl onions and mushrooms are perfect.'

'Thanks. I had time to marinate the meat in wine sauce. It makes a difference. So, has he really told the public all there is to know about the case? How very disappointing.'

'My team are not much further ahead, if I'm honest,' St. Just told her. 'No solid idea about the motive and too many suspects, if one is forced to consider disgruntled students who may have crossed the master's path. But the public doesn't need to know that. No need to cement our reputations as clueless. Of course, there's no stopping the social media commentators.'

'The true crime people, right. They're already out there in droves.'

'Are they naming names?'

'Oh, yes.' The chandelier earrings she favoured moved against her long neck as she nodded.

His heart sank. He didn't want to wade into that swamp, but he'd have to send someone off to listen in. Once in a while – a great while – the podcasters caught an angle the police hadn't considered.

'The reporter, LaFarge, seems to think it's an art theft case.'

'Does he? And there's no need for us to continue investigating, is there?'

'It's not art theft? Considering who the master was, it's a natural assumption.'

'It could be anything. Revenge, a love affair gone wrong, a random murder for a lark. There's no telling, really. Right now, yes, my money would be on murder in the commission of a theft. The man seemed to have had no enemies. No close friends either. His relationships appeared to be somewhat transactional – related to his work, I mean. He was respected in his field. Perhaps not loved, but well-liked. He wasn't the kind of man deliberately to cause friction, so far as I know.'

'Did he have any family?'

'No,' said St. Just, reaching for the butter knife. 'That's a bit sad, really. They had trouble notifying next of kin because there turned out to be no next of kin. I suppose a third cousin thrice removed may turn up one day, but so far, no. The fellows at the college are stepping up *in loco parentis*, as it were, to deal with the funeral arrangements and so on once the body is released.'

'But how terrible. We'll have to go to the service for him.'

St. Just paused to consider the ethics of that suggestion but only briefly. Portia was right. The man had no one apart from his colleagues in academia, and in fact, it was a due sign of respect for St. Just to attend. When the coroner gave the go-ahead, of course.

If the case weren't solved by that point, the chapel might, in fact, be dotted with undercover police keeping an eye on attendees. Quite famously, murderers tended to show up on these occasions. Why? No one really knew. To see the results of their handiwork? To gloat? Or more likely because their absence would be noted. Anyone deliberately not attending who should be there raises questions.

Aloud he said, 'Nice idea.'

She took a sip of wine and said, 'Maurice was right.'

'Who is Maurice?'

'Wine-seller Maurice. You know. Owns that store in town. The Goblet. He really knows his wines.'

'I'd agree.'

'Tell me more about the newspaper reporter,' she said, propping her chin on one hand. 'One podcaster has him on her list of suspects.'

St. Just topped up his glass of wine. After one sip he took a closer look at the label. French, of course.

'Yes. Barnard LaFarge got involved in a tangential way. He's not really a suspect. At least, he has what is to my mind the perfect alibi for the night of the crime. He was doing something memorable – visiting his mother in a care home in Norfolk – and staying at an inn. He probably has a receipt for the inn, but he doesn't seem to have gone out of his way to surround himself with people the entire time – at least, he didn't offer to give me an hourly accounting of witnesses and cameras and such. Only someone who knows he's going to need an alibi goes to that sort of trouble.'

'Did he strike you as honest? Because in any of the crime books I write, a suspect who is absent from the picture doing something wholesome like visiting his mother, especially, is probably working in an extra hour to dash back and do the deed.'

'I follow you,' said St. Just, 'but for one thing, a sixty-mile

trip one way is one hundred- and twenty-miles round trip.
You'd have to allow for over two hours. He couldn't just dash
back and forth. The time he arrived at his mother's nursing
home and so on will have to be checked out eventually, but I
don't see it as a priority. He claims not to have seen a good
image of any of the paintings in question, so it's hard to risk
your life over something so dubious.'

'He claims.'

'Right. We do an awful lot of taking people at their word.
By the way, he's writing a crime novel.'

'In my experience, everyone is writing a crime novel.
Especially reporters.'

'I can fend him off, if you like. Certainly, until we close
this case. I can't create a conflict of interest. He'll want an
intro to your editor and there's no telling what he might do
to get it.'

'I don't mind, honestly. When, as you say, the case is closed.
Anyway, he wrote this article about an artwork that might be
a Rembrandt – oh, of course, you've seen the article. It would
be quite the scoop if that's true.'

'Yes, it would.'

'There's a motive there.'

An outlandish one, thought St. Just, but wisely kept the
thought to himself. Besides, Portia was so often right about
these things.

'So tell me more,' she said. 'Who are your other suspects?'

'Portia, after Cornwall, we had an agreement. Remember?'

He was referring to their recent holiday in Cornwall, which
had turned into a busman's holiday. Portia had taken the initia-
tive in getting involved in a murder case, and only her quick
thinking had allowed her to escape unharmed.

'I know you're a crime writer, and a good one, but—'

'Don't say it,' she said. 'Fiction writing is quite good training
for solving crimes in real life, thank you very much. I do tons
of research to get things right in my books. But I think you're
forgetting I also lecture in criminology.'

'I'm not forgetting that for a moment. I'm just saying you're
not paid to solve crimes, and I am. But that's not really the
point. The point is it's dangerous work, and you know it.

Sometimes the less you know the better off you are. *I* need to know you're safe.'

St. Just had gone through a horrible and prolonged period of widowerhood before he met Portia, not caring very much whether he lived or died. But when Portia came into his life during a murder case in Scotland, he realized he cared very much indeed – about her safety as well as his own.

'I would argue that exactly the opposite is true,' she was saying in her low, melodious voice. 'What if I wander into a suspect's den unknowingly? Without a clue, so to speak.'

'Portia . . .'

'Don't worry. I have no intention of getting involved in the investigation. I'm so busy right now. That doesn't mean we can't discuss it a little more over dinner.' She smiled, encouragingly. 'Let's start with the painting. Is it?'

'Is it what?' He stalled.

'Is it a Rembrandt?'

'I've really no idea. The curator who was trying to get it authenticated—'

'Ambrose Nussknacker.'

'Right. He didn't have a good image of it to show. And since it may be an undiscovered masterpiece, there's no telling. I mean, if there's no record of it to begin with, it's difficult to know where to start looking. If it's what it purports to be, a true masterpiece – well, the game's afoot, I suppose. I only know it's a depiction of a young girl or woman.'

'Yes, I thought it was odd that a news story about a work of art didn't include a photo or image of the artwork. But what you say makes sense. It hadn't been properly documented or catalogued.'

'The whole subject is a bit clouded by the fact the painting was one of a cache of paintings, and those appeared to be by amateur artists. Anything's possible, early days yet. I doubt it's a matter of instant analysis, any more than are DNA results. We just have to wait.'

'Any guesses what the painting's worth?'

'If it's real? An undiscovered Rembrandt? Difficult to count that high.'

'Yes. Recently a pair of Rembrandts were found tucked

away in an attic in an old manor house belonging to some
distinguished family or other. They had no idea what they had.
They called in an appraiser to evaluate various things in the
house and lo and behold. The two paintings sold for something
over eleven million pounds.'

'So, worth killing someone over. To a person with a certain
cast of mind. I mean, there's no question eleven million would
be a temptation. The problem with all these art thefts is you
can become a bit stuck with the goods.'

Outside, a gentle patter of rain began on the windows,
adding a soothing, rhythmic soundtrack. He paused for a sip
of wine.

'I know what you mean,' said Portia. 'The problem for the
thief becomes how to sell them on. How to cash in on the
crime.'

'Exactly,' he said. 'In most cases, say a theft from an art
museum, the painting or work of art is so well known that
having stolen it, they can't unload it. There are very few dodgy
billionaires in the world who would want to get involved in
purchasing stolen art, however deep their collection mania
may run. So, potentially there's a thief stuck with something
he can't get rid of. The real danger, of course, being that they
will destroy a priceless work of art rather than let anyone else
find them with it.'

'That is how they feared a lot of art would go missing
during the Holocaust, of course. People rescued what they
could, but . . .'

'Yes, remember *The Monuments Men*?'

She nodded. 'George Clooney film. They tried to salvage
what they could of the art stolen by the Nazis on behalf of
Hitler.'

'Who saw himself as an art connoisseur.'

'Deciding what works were "degenerate". Utter madness.'

'There are probably unknown treasures still to be found,'
said St. Just. 'Of course, the works that were destroyed or lost
to bombings or to cover up their theft are gone forever.'

Portia nodded. 'My colleague at the institute will be all over
this. She might be a useful resource for your investigation.'

'She might. What's her name again?'

'Annalise Bellagamba,' said Portia.

'Yes, of course, LaFarge quoted her in his article, didn't he?'

'There's barely an article written on art theft that doesn't mention her, really. She does a lot of work with MI5 and MI6, consulting on stolen art.'

'I'll keep that in mind; she may be useful to us. Once we find out where the painting has got to. Let alone, which direction we're going with the murder case.'

'She's in Poland now. She's working with curators to rescue whatever art they were able to salvage from Ukraine. But she'll be back this week.'

He sat back in his chair. 'Great, I'll let you know. That was a delicious meal, by the way.'

'Thank you. It's easy, really. Just takes a bit of time. And now you're safely home and fed, I've got some prep work to do for tomorrow's sessions.'

'I'm going to catch the news headlines before I write up my notes from today. Maybe make a few calls. Then off to bed. I hope the phone doesn't ring in the middle of the night.'

'For both our sakes,' she said, but with a smile.

'I'm glad you're getting a firsthand view of what life will be like once we're married.'

'Oh, you mean the middle-of-the-night phone calls won't magically stop?'

'I'm afraid not. You're not changing your mind, are you?'

He was joking, but he could never quite mask his darkest fear: Portia would wake up one day and realize she could have had any man she wanted instead of a hard-working, largely absentee policeman. He tried not to question miracles, and this was surely one. Their lives were so seamlessly blended it was hard to say any more where he stopped and Portia began.

And her beauty? It took his breath away.

St. Just did not think of himself as handsome. His most distinguishing characteristic was his size. He was often described as 'that large policeman'. He came from Cornish stock, and had in an idle moment traced his roots to somewhere near Penwith, but he was tall so perhaps had a dash of French pirate thrown in. Not necessarily overweight, just . . . large. Tall and broad.

Perhaps, he thought ruefully, getting a bit broader. Sometimes contentment did that to a man.

'Arthur, never,' Portia was saying. 'I could ask the same of you, you know.'

'Are you serious? I would have to be mad not to want you in my life. You make it worth living.'

'And there you have it. I feel the same.'

There was a beat while they sat beaming at each other, and Portia poured the last of the wine. Then she said, 'So who will you be interviewing first tomorrow?'

'Portia, you are my life, but I need you to stay out of it.'

'I'll arrange a meeting with Annalise, at least.'

'Fine. If I have specific questions for her by then. I don't want to waste her time. Now, let's talk about something else. How about we finally sort out a date for our wedding?'

'You know as well as I do if we name a date, it's guaranteed someone will be murdered on that date.' She thought a moment, adding, 'There's something a bit uncanny about it, this trail of murders we seem to create just by our being in the area – like what happened in Cornwall. Now I've said it aloud, I know it to be true. It doesn't matter if we simply elope, or get married in our own living room, something will happen to someone.'

'Then someone else will have to investigate it. I'm not indispensable.'

'But you are. You know you are. To me and to the police. Maybe when you retire?'

'There's no way I'm waiting to marry you until I retire.'

Besides, he thought, I doubt that would stop the murders. As Portia had said, murder seemed to turn up for them like a bad penny, and not just because of his job as a crime-solver. The crime spree had really got going when he met Portia. *Superstitious nonsense.*

Aloud he said, 'We'll figure it out. Maybe in summer term, when you're less busy?'

'I'll pencil you in for a June wedding.'

TEN

HQ

The next morning St. Just drove to the headquarters of the Cambridgeshire Constabulary, located in Huntingdon outside the city of Cambridge proper. There were times when even the constant exchange of information by text and email could not substitute for the old face-to-face meeting.

A mild sun broke through the clouds as he pulled the car into his reserved spot before making his way to his office in the far reaches of the building. The place was meant to inspire awe and good conduct from the populace, but it somehow failed to look like anything but a car park that had been converted to office space. St. Just spent as much time away from his desk there as he could manage.

Sergeant Fear was on the job already. St. Just could never tell if Fear was supremely dedicated or welcomed the chance for a break from his all-consuming family life. He was a dedicated father, St. Just was certain, but his way of showing dedication was to make sure he got promoted so he could take better care of his family.

Despite his solid recommendations, St. Just had been unable to hoist his faithful sidekick into a higher pay grade. There was a danger Sergeant Fear would seek greener pastures, chasing after a promotion, and that had to be prevented at any cost. He needed him here, by his side.

He had already instructed Fear to call a meeting in the squad room so he could take reports from the various team members. Ten in all had by now been assigned to the case. That was a generous allotment – the chief had slotted the case into a priority folder – but it would never be enough people to cover every detail that needed to be investigated quickly.

Still, one of the officers interviewing witnesses had managed to discover that Sir Flyte had attended a formal dinner at another college the previous evening, helping to plot the master's whereabouts in the hours leading to his death.

Unfortunately, St. Just had learned little from an email that morning from the pathologist, Dr Pomeroy. Forensics had not come up with anything startlingly new, although the time of death had been tightened to being an hour on either side of 11:30 p.m., and they already knew that the master was dead at midnight. Pomeroy had further written, in the plain-English or 'Autopsies for Dummies' part of his report:

> *There are a total of four incised wounds present on the deceased's back. All wounds exhibit characteristics consistent with a sharp-edged, pointed instrument. The clean-cut margins, linear shape, and the presence of minor abrasions surrounding each wound suggest a single forceful penetration with the pointed end, followed by a slicing motion with the blade for each wound.*
>
> *The first wound, located in the mid-thoracic region, approximately 5cm to the left of the spinal column, penetrated vital structures, specifically the left lung and the aorta. Given the location and depth of this wound, it is likely to have been the cause of rapid blood loss, leading to rapid respiratory distress and circulatory collapse.*
>
> *The subsequent three wounds do not appear to have directly involved any major vascular structures or organs to the extent of the first wound. Their positioning, depth, and angles of entry suggest they might have been inflicted in rapid succession following the first wound.*
>
> *While all four wounds are consistent with the described weapon and would have caused significant injury, the first wound is the most likely to be the immediate cause of the victim's demise. The nature and positioning of the wounds and the position of the body at the scene further suggest a potential surprise attack from behind while the victim was seated.*

'As usual, it's give-or-take on that timeline,' Dr Pomeroy had told St. Just in their follow-up call. 'But death was as close to instantaneous as any of us could wish for. Sir Flyte was a man in his mid-sixties presenting no evidence or history of medical issues or drug use but, of course, medical issues don't lead to a knife being plunged into one's back. The same can't be said for illicit drug use, of course, given the people drawn into that world, but Sir Flyte was not abusing his system with anything more potent than wine. He had the equivalent of a large glass in his system, and that's all.'

'I heard from one of my team late last night he had dined out at another college,' St. Just told him. 'A call from the master there got relayed to her.'

'Yes, he had had rather a large meal. Would you like to hear about the stomach contents?'

'No. But the wine – that's interesting,' said St. Just.

'Is it? Why?'

'These high-table affairs generally involve a lot of wine with dinner, and then there's the after-dinner business of more drinking. He must have been conspicuously abstemious compared with his colleagues.'

'Perhaps he was. There's certainly no sign of chronic alcohol abuse. For his age he was fit and might have been looking at a good twenty years' more life to come. What's interesting to me is the four stab wounds, the first one undoubtedly fatal, the others just to make absolutely sure. That leads me to believe this was not a frenzied attack but a methodical one.'

'Wouldn't the perpetrator have had *some* blood on him after stabbing the man four times?'

'As I told you at the scene, there would likely be some blood spatter, even if microscopic. Unless he or she took care to wear something to cover their clothing, in which case we may be out of luck. I would say whoever did this wasn't the type to panic or fail to think ahead. Except the weapon was probably a letter opener or a paper knife, and that seems improvised.'

'A letter opener . . .'

'That's my best guess. With a sharp blade. I've no advice on the exact weapon used, as no weapon was found at the scene. In other words, there's no letter opener left on the master's desk conveniently covered in his blood and with the perpetrator's fingerprints and DNA on it, but that's not conclusive. The master may not have used a letter opener in his work – letter openers mostly went the way of the dodo anyway, with the dawn of email – so whoever did have an object like that, they may have brought the weapon with them.'

'Or simply taken it with them when they left. And later thrown it away.'

'Right. The master was murdered by someone who'd either had the forethought to bring his own weapon, or the wit to take the master's letter opener with him after he'd murdered him. Anyway, that's what I've got so far. And I have another body waiting to be looked into. So if there's nothing else . . .'

At the end of the day, did it really matter? wondered St. Just, ending the call. The poor man was dead. The possibility of his killer's wearing something to prevent being hit with blood spatter was interesting, though. It took forethought to bring an outer garb with you to commit a crime.

But it also created for the killer the problem of disposing of the protective covering, or the street clothing he or she had been wearing.

Blood never washed out entirely, as anyone watching police shows on the telly would know.

The most usual disposal site would be a fireplace or a city litter bin, but there was every chance whatever it was would never be recovered.

He relayed what he'd learned to his team, then asked: 'Was there a thorough search of the master's office?'

They looked at each other, then nodded in unison.

'Specifically, did you find the master's academic robe in the office?'

'Yes, there was a black robe hanging from a hook by the door.' This from a young Constable he'd not worked with before. The name on her tag looked like Agoraphobia, but that couldn't be right. He'd be needing bifocals soon.

'It was bagged, was it?'

'I'll find out,' she said.

'Please do, and make sure it gets to forensics. Did we get anything from a search of the area around the Master's Lodge? Outside the lodge, I mean.'

The rookie of the bunch, only six months on the job, held up his hand.

'What is it, Constable Neighbors?'

'There was nothing to suggest any break-in or entry except by key or by admittance. However, I had a word with the porter who said the master did not lock his door. No one did unless they were leaving the college for an extended period. There had not been any break-ins, not even a petty theft. It simply didn't happen.'

The constable's look of surprise said it all. Cambridge was a major city with all the attendant problems of a major city, but these colleges operated as little enclaves of peace and tranquillity. Despite what St. Just knew to be the lack of security at Hardwick College, he could understand the impulse to save money and cling to the old ways of centuries before when there was no technology to help repel invaders. The porters in those days would have been skilled in hand-to-hand combat, he was certain, and that would be all that was needed.

The night porter in this case, Oliver, could with almost a clear conscience watch the telly or take a nap or whatever he did during the wee hours of the morning. No one would've expected what happened to the master to happen. In fact, St. Just paused, wondering if a master had ever been murdered in his lodgings in centuries past. Maybe when the case was over, he'd Google the topic.

'Anything turning up from a search of the Master's Lodge itself? The upstairs?'

This was answered by another new addition to the team, this time one he recognized. Constable Rachel Broadhurst.

'It was an easy search,' she said. 'The master was a methodical man. Clothes neatly folded, nothing thrown about. His study was the only place where he seemed to let his hair down a bit, but even then, I'm sure it was the kind of organizational system used by many, including myself. He knew where he had left things so he could find them again, even if no one else could.'

'Did you find a painting of a young woman – a painting in the style of Rembrandt?'

'I'm sure not. I'll check my inventory list but I'd remember something like that.'

'So, were there any indications of debt or some other unhappiness that had crept into his life? Did anyone run the financials on him?'

It was Sergeant Patel, who had a reputation for being able to spot the pattern or flaw in any spreadsheet, who said, 'His financials are in good order. In fact, he had very recently inherited some money and a house from his aunt. She lived in a small village and left him her life savings. It didn't amount to a huge windfall, but I'm sure it would pay for a few holidays in Majorca.'

'Apart from that, no large sums deposited or withdrawn from the bank, then?' St. Just had assumed the master wouldn't be involved in any kind of skulduggery, but one never knew. He was often surrounded by priceless works of art, being asked to evaluate them. He would rub shoulders with people in high places with grand possessions. Maybe there was temptation there, and one day the temptation might have been too great. He might have offered to take a 'worthless' painting off someone's hands for a song, then later resold it to the highest bidder.

But barring some extreme and sudden need for cash, that suggested conduct at odds with what he knew of the master's character.

The lack of suspicious activity in his accounts seemed to rule out anything like blackmail, and it was even harder to picture such a man being blackmailed. Then again, he was in high office and a highly respected one. The threat of exposure of any kind would not be met with the old 'publish and be damned' retort. A man in his shoes, St. Just felt, would pay up and hope the blackmailer never came back for seconds.

'I need someone to get me a copy of any important papers found in his office. I believe the inventory mentioned a briefcase. I'll have copies of the contents of that.'

'On it, guv,' said Constable Broadhurst.

Thoughts of the master's gown made him think of Rufus Penn and his untidy room. He wouldn't have been surprised to learn Rufus's academic gown was being carelessly used as a bathrobe.

He decided to have another word with Mr Rufus Penn of upstate New York. Their last conversation had left him with a feeling the young man knew more than he was saying.

St. Just ended the meeting, signalled Sergeant Fear, and went to find Rufus before he had a chance to disappear into one of the university's many libraries for the day.

ELEVEN
Dinner at Eight

They found Rufus just returned to his rooms from breakfast in Hall. Reluctantly he admitted them, having made clear with a theatrical sigh that the novelty of being interviewed by the police was wearing thin.

'We are here because you seem to have remarkable powers of observation for one so young,' said St. Just. 'I wonder if you could describe for us the dinner you were invited to that evening – the evening of the night the master died.'

'Was murdered, you mean,' said Rufus Penn. 'Why didn't you tell me that in the first place?'

'We have our methods,' said St. Just obscurely. 'What was talked about, anything unusual that happened, anything at all you noticed. Would you mind taking those bud things out of your ears? Thank you.'

Sergeant Fear kept his eyes firmly on his notebook. Rufus Penn's 'remarkable powers of observation' seemed to be focused mainly on himself. But the blatant flattery was a tried-and-true technique of St. Just's. It often worked. The larger the ego, the more often it worked.

'There was nothing unusual about it,' said Penn, taking the flattery in his stride. 'And I really must insist—'

'Everything that night was unusual,' said St. Just mildly. 'When a murder is involved, nothing is ordinary. Again, I'm sure that you would notice anything amiss, out of all the people at the table at this dinner party. Let's go through it again in more detail. Who was with you at this meal?'

He knew the answer, but he wanted to give Rufus Penn's mind room to roam and hopefully wander off the established path. Even better, for him to contradict anything he'd said before. St. Just would give him every opportunity to put his personality on display.

'Well, all right. There were only four of us, as I said before. There was Dr Pat, the woman in charge of women's studies.'

'By that you must mean Professor Patricia Beadle-Batsford, head of the university's Department of Women's Studies.'

'Right. Quite famous, as I understand it. I must say, it's not an area I know a lot about.'

In his notebook, Sergeant Fear wrote down the remark and underlined it. Next to it he wrote: *I'll bet.*

'Then there was Ambrose Nussknacker. I've also told you this before. He's a curator of a little museum and art gallery up on Castle Hill. He is an entertaining guy and, of course, with both him and me at the table, the conversation ranged over our areas of interest.'

'I'm sure the ladies enjoyed that,' said St. Just.

Any irony flew straight over Penn's head. Clearly the women's enjoyment was not of interest to him.

'And then there was Peyton. That's it, just the four of us.'

'I understand you and Peyton have been seeing something of each other.'

'Do you? She's simply a friend.'

'I understood you were romantically involved,' said St. Just, fishing.

'Nothing could be further from the truth,' insisted Penn. 'She is a nice-looking girl, of course, but the world is full of nice-looking girls and the night is young, in a manner of speaking. *I* am young.'

'Quite wise you are,' said St. Just, thinking such young men should come with a warning. Lock up your daughters, indeed. The man-to-man tone was grating. Penn was talking to two men in long-term, happy relationships. St. Just felt young Rufus should learn to read the room better.

'So, walk us through what happened. I'm more interested in the time leading up to when the dinner ended, unless something unusual happened during dinner.'

'Nothing unusual,' said Penn. 'There was quite a lot of drinking. I will say this for Pat, she keeps an a-*maz*-ing wine cellar for such a small house.'

'It sounds as if you are on friendly terms.'

'How do you mean?'

'I mean that it's probably quite rare for her to be addressed as Pat or even Dr Pat by a student. And rarer still that she wouldn't take offence. I'm sure she earned those titles. So, she doesn't live in college?'

Again, he knew the answer from the briefings he'd read on all the people who had some connection to the night's events, but it was more edifying to hear things from Penn's point of view. As someone coming from outside the UK, he might also have a different perspective.'

'Oh, no. She has a house to the east of town, one of those Victorian-era workmen's places that now sell for a tidy sum.'

'So. There was a lot of talk and laughter? Quite a bit of drinking?'

'It was an enjoyable evening,' admitted Penn after a pause. 'Yes.'

'And then all of you left to return to Cambridge proper? Did you walk?'

'Pey stayed behind.'

'Peyton, the daughter?'

'Right. Ambrose offered me a ride back to the college. He dropped me off at the front gate on his way home.'

At a nod from St. Just, Sergeant Fear read aloud from his notes: '"Ambrose dropped me back at the college about eleven. I went out for a drink and returned after midnight to this commotion around the Master's Lodge."'

St. Just asked, 'Do you stand by that statement?'

He and Fear exchanged brief glances, both having made the same calculation: the night porter might have seen him enter at any time between eleven and when the porter hared off to investigate at midnight. The porter might be a witness, in other words, but only *if* Rufus entered through the front gate. St. Just knew from his student days that there was more than one way into these old buildings.

'Of course I do,' said Rufus.

'And no one at the college saw you return. The porter?'

'They were all standing about looking at the Master's Lodge. I don't know if they saw me or not.'

Fair play. But with all the selfies being taken that night someone might accidently have photographed him. St. Just would make sure crowd photos were mentioned in any further emails going out to staff and students. Surely there'd been dozens of mobile photos taken before he'd ordered his team to widen the cordon.

'You say the curator returned to his home. Where is that?'

'I have no idea where it might be. Up the hill near the museum would be my guess. He struck me as a man married to his museum.'

'And what time was this?'

'Oh, ten forty-five. Maybe closer to eleven.'

'Perhaps after eleven?'

'Maybe. I wasn't paying attention.'

Interesting, thought St. Just. His time of return to the college might place him right in the thick of things, as far as murder was concerned. A guilty man would have fudged the time a bit more. Still, few people can account for every minute of their doings, especially after a drinks-fuelled dinner.

But perhaps Penn was a step ahead, knowing that others would be asked about the time in question, and he wouldn't want his testimony to conflict with theirs.

'I decided to go for a nightcap. To the Saracen's Head. They have a licence to stay open well past the usual eleven p.m. closing for pubs. Loads of people saw me there. I might have a time-stamped photo or two, even.'

He grabbed his mobile and scrolled through a few photos. 'Here, have a look.'

He handed the phone to St. Just. Rufus seemed to have wasted no time in making new friends in the UK. Several photos featured a girl or two hanging off his arm or draped casually around his shoulders. He wondered what Peyton would make of this.

He handed the phone to Sergeant Fear, saying, 'Make a note of those times.'

But the photos seemed to clear Rufus. St. Just recognized the interior of the pub, so there was no question that was where he was.

'And what time did you leave the pub?'

'At midnight when it closed. The bartender called closing,

so I paid up . . . Oh! I'll have a time-stamped receipt for that somewhere, too. In my phone app.'

St. Just was reminded of what he'd said to Portia the night before. The person who doesn't realize he'll need an alibi tends to have the most believable alibi.

'Anyway, I walked back to the college and got to the gates after midnight. Maybe fifteen or twenty minutes past? There was already a huddle of people in their nightclothes standing about, a bit of a police presence. The porter stood looking like he'd had the stuffing knocked out of him.'

'The gates were unlocked? The main gate?'

'Yeah. I was thinking I'd have to climb over the wall, but I guess in all the hubbub the porter forgot. The outer gates were standing wide open.'

'Why did it take you so long to get back to the college? It can't be much more than a five-minute walk from the Saracen's Head to Hardwick.'

'I kind of lost track of time. I'd met this girl named Daphne and I walked her to her door. She's invited me to a dinner at her college next week. She has my email, so I can get her last name for you when she writes, if you need to know. Am I a suspect?'

Such confidence! Of course Daphne would write.

'Not unless the photos you showed us have been doctored. Or the receipt.'

Sergeant Fear shook his head. Unless Rufus was some mastermind computer guru, they would have to accept the testimony of the time-stamps. And of the all-too-human Daphne, if it came to that.

'Let's get back to the dinner at Professor Patricia Beadle-Batsford's house. Again, nothing unusual happened, in your memory of events? What did you do after the meal?'

Penn seemed to hesitate. 'Well, Ambrose and I retired to the garden for a cigar while the women cleared the table.'

'You didn't offer to help?'

'No.' The suggestion seemed to astound him. 'I was a guest.'

Whether or not Penn offered to help was a slightly nonsensical question under the circumstances, but St. Just was taken aback by the reply. What century were they living in?

'All right. And what did you and Ambrose Nussknacker talk about in the garden?'

'He mentioned a bit of conflict he was having with the master. A rather serious clash of views about AI, like I said before. Quite serious. But you'd have to ask him.'

Well, that was Penn once again smoothly landing Ambrose in the potentially dangerous waters of having been in conflict with the master.

Well done, thought St. Just. He may as well have come flat out and accused Ambrose of threatening to kill the master.

'And Peyton?'

'Peyton what?'

'She didn't return to the college with you and Ambrose?'

'No, she stayed at home. She lives with her mother since she dropped out of college.'

'Is that how you met her? When she was a student at Cambridge?'

'Yes. At a gathering for new students. She didn't last long. Talks a lot of nonsense about how life is the best teacher, not the classroom. I suppose that makes sense if all you want to do is wait tables and travel the world, but . . . not for me.'

'The wanderer's life, or Peyton herself?'

'Both, I suppose. Peyton can be a bit . . . clingy.'

'And, what about Peyton? Was she enjoying the evening?'

Penn shrugged. 'I guess. She didn't say much. She had cooked the dinner and was flitting about getting the different courses. They don't have staff. Quite surprising. I thought all Cambridge dons had at least a butler.'

Sergeant Fear's pen flew across the page. St. Just could just imagine the editorial comments.

'Perhaps you're thinking of Lord Peter Wimsey's valet Bunter. How were the mother and daughter getting along?'

No doubt the daughter's dropping out of college would be a source of contention for any parent. Especially for a parent so invested in the academic life.

'I don't know. I'm sure Pey needed to find a new place to live pretty soon. Her mother wouldn't want the free room and board to go on indefinitely. I guess I can't blame her. Pey can be a handful.'

'In what way?'

'I can't really say.'

'You can, you know. What is it? Is it drugs?'

'I honestly don't think so. Not to any degree. Her body is her temple, all that sort of thing. Look, I have a follow-up supervision with Professor Bailey, and I need to prepare.'

'Bailey! Good heavens, is he still around?'

'You know him?'

'Yes, I know him. They had a nickname for him in my day.'

'Yes,' said Penn, with his first real grin since they'd started the interview. 'The Old Bailey, they call him. It's a well-earned name. He doesn't so much enlighten his students as terrify them into agreeing with him.'

'Right. Some things never change. Well, we won't keep you for now, Rufus – if I may – but anything you remember later might be important. Especially since you arrived back at college so near the time we think the master was killed. But between the dinner and the pub your time seems to be accounted for.' This was not strictly true, but someone would be verifying his movements between the time of his leaving the dinner party with Ambrose, being dropped off at Hardwick, arriving at the pub, and leaving it with Daphne. The same would be true for Ambrose's whereabouts after the party.

Penn made a little action imitating a shiver.

'It's terrible to think about, really. Him being killed. Now if there is nothing else—'

'Did you see the porter as you entered?'

'I told you. The porter was there, not looking great.'

He had, but St. Just still had the urge to probe Rufus for inconsistencies.

'All right, I think that's all.' St. Just looked to Sergeant Fear for confirmation, and all three men rose from their seats. 'You can say hello to Professor Bailey for me when you see him. He may remember.'

'Old Bailey was your supervisor? You read art history?'

'I attended many of his lectures. I heard later he was distressed to hear I'd gone into police work. To him it was as if I'd taken up stock lending or accounting. For men like Bailey, the arts are all that matter.'

'It is a bit of a leap to policing. What made you do it?'

It was the first moment in the interview that Penn had shown interest in someone else's doings than his own, so St. Just answered honestly.

'I saw things in the world going so wrong I didn't think even art and beauty could touch them. I feared that soon there would be nothing left for us to cherish. And I wanted to see if I could change that.'

'No kidding?'

'No kidding. Good luck with Professor Bailey.'

As they were leaving, St. Just headed upstairs rather than down. Sergeant Fear, never questioning, followed him up the stone steps, which became narrower as they climbed. Clearly, the stairwell had been designed for medieval frames. Fear himself was slight in build but St. Just was large. Fear had a wild thought they might have to get the fire brigade to extract him if the walls narrowed much further.

They reached the top, and St. Just asked to borrow the small torch attached to Fear's keychain. Aiming its light at the ceiling, St. Just said, 'It is as I thought. There's a way up to the roof through here. And it's been used recently, or else the cleaning staff is quite thorough. There are none of the cobwebs or dirt I'd expect to see.'

'You think someone's getting access to the roof, then,' said Fear. 'But why?'

'Oh, I don't know. To enjoy the clear night air as a little escape from studying, or as a hideaway for anyone romantically inclined. Or for the more adventurous, perhaps a bit of sky-walking.'

'*Sky-walking*. But . . . that's been banned for years. Don't tell me students are still doing it.'

'Of course they are. It's child's play to access and crawl about on some of these old roofs. I did it myself as an undergraduate.'

'You did?'

'Yes.'

Sergeant Fear stared at him a long moment.

'You needn't look so astonished, Sergeant. I was quite . . . quite daring in my day.'

'No offence, sir.'

'None taken. Lighter on my feet, too, you know. Positively balletic.'

'It's just that never in my wildest dreams did I picture you as some sort of cat burglar. Just wait until I tell the wife.'

'A better word than "daring" might be "stupid". We called it night-climbing back then because we did it under cover of darkness. They call it buildering now – especially when it's done on tall monuments. Or as you say, sky-walking, when they leap from one rooftop to another. Insanely dangerous, of course.

'The colleges are child's play in comparison to the Eiffel Tower, but it's still a terrible idea.'

TWELVE
Peyton

'I suppose we should talk to Peyton and her mother,' said St. Just. 'With any luck, we'll find them together and kill two birds. Her mother might work from home on occasion.'

Sergeant Fear looked up the address and entered it into the GPS. It was a short drive to the house where the dinner party had been held. St. Just timed it, in fact. It came to seven minutes in traffic. It would take five minutes, he calculated, in the dead of night.

As Rufus Penn had said, the house was in what had been a working-class part of town, but like its neighbours it had been tarted up – probably converted from a boarding house – and now might go for a tidy sum.

A girl they assumed was Peyton opened the door as they parked in front of the house. She seemed to have been expecting them. They strode to the door and flashed their warrant cards.

She was one of these young women who looked to St. Just to be fifteen going on forty. A pretty girl, if a bit unformed: the outlines of her face had not quite hardened into adulthood and were soft and rounded, her features mobile, her eyelashes unapologetically false. Her mother, she explained, was at work.

'She's always at work,' said Peyton. It sounded like an old refrain. 'Doesn't she need to be here when I'm being interviewed?'

'Not at all. You're not a minor, are you?'

'Am I a suspect?'

Somehow, St. Just hadn't been expecting this. 'No,' he said. 'Should you be?'

'You're not going to issue me a warning or something?'

'No, miss. But I'm glad you're up on your television viewing. *Line of Duty* is riveting, isn't it? They've really captured the police jargon. I wonder if half the viewers know what they're saying. For the record, we rarely talk to each other like that, not when plain English will do. Do we, Sergeant Fear?'

'Roger that,' said Fear. 'Ten-four.'

She didn't seem entirely sure they were kidding. Cops on the telly didn't often lark about – too busy running after suspects – and they didn't tend to make house calls, either. She made no move to admit them and St. Just decided not to press it.

'Well, what is it then?'

At least she made no pretence of having somewhere else to be. Her attitude was that of a person with time on her hands, in fact. All the time in the world.

This led St. Just to his next question. 'You are no longer a student at Hardwick College, I understand.'

'Not for me,' she said with a dismissive wave. 'I can learn more things about the world at a restaurant than I will ever learn in one of those stuffy supervisions.'

Sergeant Fear didn't seem to be taking this well. St. Just could gauge his reactions without a glance at this point, after so many years in harness. The privilege that allowed the girl to toss away a first-rate education without a backward glance was galling. He was certain her justification would be that it was a waste of money.

'It's just a waste of money,' she said. 'I didn't want to put my mother through that.'

Something about that last sentiment rang false.

'Surely she didn't begrudge you the money?'

'She would have if I'd been sent down. I thought I'd spare us all the drama.'

'I see. So, you are working as a waitress, I gather?'

'I work at a restaurant,' she answered vaguely.

'Name?'

'Virtue.'

'I worked as a bartender at night when I was a student.'

'Really?' This from a startled Sergeant Fear. This was for him a day of revelations. First sky-walking, now working in a bar. Whatever next?

'Really,' said St. Just. 'You are right – you learn to handle people at their best and their worst. You also get rather used to hearing confessions. It was, I suppose, good training for being a policeman. But I wouldn't trade my grounding in academics for anything. You never know until years later how valuable that broad experience is. Maybe you'll return and pick up your studies one day. But, of course, this is not why we are here.'

'Yes, exactly why are you here?' She batted the eyelashes, a flicker of annoyance.

He thought how best to frame the question without directly implicating Ambrose Nussknacker. Failing to find a way, he chose to step round her question.

'I understand there was a dinner party here, and as it ended about the time the master met his end, I will need a few more details.'

She wasn't falling for it. 'Surely you'll end up interviewing the entire city of Cambridge at this rate. Are you going to find out everyone's whereabouts at midnight? It's hardly a manor-house mystery, is it?'

'You'd be surprised,' he said. 'Would you mind cooperating by telling us what you recall of the evening?' There was a tone to his voice implying a veiled but empty threat: it might go better for her if she cooperated.

'Well, you may as well come in and sit down then,' she said, adopting an offhand attitude. But St. Just detected a certain excitement beneath it all, a certain glimmer in her eyes. He'd seen this before with true crime aficionados.

Inwardly, he sighed. She was going to offer them help whether they wanted it or not, as well as fabrications if she saw an opening.

She guided them towards a sitting room that had been updated for modern tastes. All drapey Victorian furniture had been banished in favour of a warm Nordic vibe. There were patterned pillows thrown about on a nubby oatmeal sofa and matching chairs. The whole was arranged before a brick fire-place with a tile surround.

'Would you like some coffee?' she asked.

Her initial defensiveness seemed to have melted. This was

possibly the most exciting thing that had happened to her since she left college, unless her restaurant had had a kitchen fire. Murder did that to people, even murder at second remove.

'Do you know, I think I will say yes to that.' He looked at Sergeant Fear.

Sergeant Fear said, 'Ta very much.'

Like Barnard LaFarge, Peyton wore the torn jeans that had become ubiquitous in the past few years. St. Just had asked Portia what that trend was about, since to him it was a baffling choice. She had said she thought it had something to do with showing solidarity with people who had no choice but to wear torn clothing, or perhaps it was some kind of sexual thing. Or possibly to do with recycling to save the planet – she really couldn't say. She did comment that once Hollywood stars adopted the style, it was time for everyone to move on.

Peyton's hair was dyed blonde, cut in a thick, sharp wedge to chin length round an oval face. His guess was it had been an expensive job. But dark brown hair was starting to grow out at the roots, so perhaps her mother's generosity stopped at room and board. Or maybe showing roots was another fashion trend. It was so hard to keep up.

They settled into the comfortable room and waited for the coffee. It was unusual for St. Just to accept such an offer, but he wanted the chance to send Fear out on a brief mission to explore at least the lower floor of the house. He doubted they'd have time for the upper floor.

Sergeant Fear returned not a moment too soon, mere seconds before Peyton came clattering into the room with a tray. Since he was already standing, Fear took the tray from her and set it down on the coffee table.

She sorted them out with milk and sugar and biscuits, and they sat back, looking for all the world as if they were in a Swedish vicarage having a chat about the upcoming fundraiser.

'So what is it you need to know? I've been thinking already about the usual police questioning, which would be, was anything out of the ordinary happening at the meal? And the answer would be no. I cooked quite a good beef bourguignon with mushrooms, as it happened. We had good wine from the cellar. My mother is a bit of a, well, let's just say it, she's a wine snob. It's from her that I learned so much about wine it got me a job at the restaurant. I plan to get certified as a sommelier one day.'

'Excellent,' said St. Just, glad that she did seem to have plans and a goal. Somehow this came as a relief.

'So if you wouldn't mind, what was the seating arrangement?'

'I'll show you before you leave, if you like (Sergeant Fear struggled to look as if this would be a novelty for him), but it's a large dining table. My mother sits at the head. The curator sat at the other end, and Rufus and I sat across from each other.'

'Quite a small party then.'

'Yes, there had been two other guests invited, a married couple. They had to bail at the last minute – a sick child or something.'

'Oh, I don't think we knew that. Could you give us their names, please, before we leave?'

'Sure, I might even have a phone number for them. It's a professor in women's studies who works for my mother, and her partner. Frankly, I was relieved they weren't going to be there. They could be a bit one-topic, if you know what I mean.'

'I don't. Could you fill us in?'

'Women's studies, of course. The oppression of women down through the centuries. Freeing women from their chains. Down with the patriarchy! Not that I disagree, really. I know there's been oppression, but this is the twenty-first century, and I don't know why they have to bang on and on about what happened so far in the past.'

'Perhaps your generation is benefiting from the protests and sacrifices of the previous generations. Besides, there are many areas of the world where women aren't even allowed to drive a car.'

'That's exactly the kind of thing my mother says.' But she smiled. 'All right, I get it. Women – generally speaking – have a lot more freedom nowadays but, quite honestly, I don't know why there isn't a men's studies. You ever think of that?'

'An argument could be made that it's been men's studies all along. White men's studies, at that. Now, did you believe their excuse for not being at the dinner? It must've been somewhat inconvenient for you to have to buy and cook for six people and then end up with only four.'

She shrugged. 'I really was happier not to have them. I love leftovers, anyway. And cooking. My mother was seldom home to cook anything that didn't come from a jar, so I taught myself.'

'It seems an odd assortment of people, in a way. How does your mother know Ambrose . . .' He paused and looked at Sergeant Fear.

'Ambrose Nussknacker,' said Fear.

'Right. Ambrose Nussknacker.'

'They were planning an exhibit at his gallery. The pandemic hit places like that hard, and a popular exhibit could give him a boost. Women artists down through the ages – you know the sort of thing. So he called on my mother to consult. She ended up inviting him for dinner. Then she thought the other women's studies people might have something to say.'

'The master of the college to which she's attached was not invited? He's *the* art expert, after all.'

She shook her head. 'No idea. I volunteered to cook the dinner, but to even out the numbers I invited my boyfriend.' A small trill of pride on the word 'boyfriend'. 'Since he was studying art history, I thought he might have an interest in the conversation. And he did. He and old Ambrose got on like the proverbial house on fire. It is good for Rufus to establish that sort of connection.'

St. Just registered the proud reference to Rufus being her boyfriend and, remembering Daphne, struggled to keep a neutral expression on his face. As he suspected, the relationship existed largely in her mind, with only Rufus knowing the endgame.

'That would be Rufus Penn, would it not?'

'Yes. Have you spoken to him? How is he doing? I mean, how is he holding up? I'm sure it's a real scandal-fest over there at the college right now.'

'I don't think he's overly concerned. He didn't know the master particularly well, did he?'

'No. But the mutual interest in art . . .' She paused. 'I don't know, probably that was why he applied to Hardwick in the first place. The master had set a high bar, you see, for expertise in art history, and that, of course, was what Rufus wanted most of all.'

'That connection to power and prestige.'

'You could put it that way.'

'How interesting,' said St. Just. 'I should have thought knowledge was what he was after.'

'That too, of course,' she said defensively. 'He is ambitious, and ambition is a good thing in a noble cause. I'm ambitious in my own way, but, well . . .'

This was the opening St. Just had been waiting for.

'I would imagine your mother's professional achievements might be a lot to live up to. I endured a certain amount of that in my upbringing.'

This was bordering on falsehood. His parents had never done anything but encourage him and think him wonderful in every way, although his turning to the police for a career had been rather unexpected. They had pulled themselves together eventually and rallied behind him, as they always did.

'I don't think that many people are aware of my mother, although, yes, I recognize she's an expert in her field.' The words 'expert in her field' were accompanied by air quotes and a mocking, teenagerish expression. 'I had no interest in any of that, from the beginning. No real interest in school, for that matter, although I did well enough. That was her life. I wanted my own life.'

'I can understand that completely. Might I ask where your father is?'

'He died. Well . . . that is to say . . .' Death was a straightforward-enough explanation, thought St. Just, but then she explained further, 'They divorced, and then he died. I was a child. I don't remember much about it. It's always been me and my mother.'

'Was he also an academic?'

'As a matter of fact, he was. Before you ask, art history. But he's long gone now. In fact, well, he was never part of my life, as I've explained.'

'Here at Cambridge?'

'Yeah. In the department over there.' She waved a hand briefly in the general direction of the building housing Cambridge's Department of Art History.

'And that didn't interest you either?'

'Funny you should ask. When Rufus came along, I was not really interested in him when he told me his field of study. He was very good-looking, but it was like, oh, no! You know the sort of thing.' She waited for acknowledgement from either of the men of their knowing the sort of thing but was met with stony silence. 'Anyway, it was a case of opposites attract, I suppose. Rufus is a force of nature, and I'll tell you what – thanks to him I've come to appreciate the art world more than I ever would have done without him. He's a genius – pure and simple. Rufus Penn is a genius.'

Sergeant Fear made a meticulous notation of this little spurt of hero worship.

'I'm glad to see you're writing that down. He'll be famous one day, mark my words.' She laughed. 'Well, I guess you just did.'

'So,' said St. Just, 'returning to that evening. It was a successful dinner party?'

'Yes,' she said. 'As I told you, I'm quite a good cook. And everything came off as planned. No bread burning in the oven, no fires or spilt milk.'

'I meant, rather,' said St. Just, 'the conversation. Was there perfect harmony? Any disagreement? What exactly was talked about?'

'Oh.' She clearly had to search her memory. St. Just imagined her attention was focused on Rufus and whether he was enjoying her cooking.

'Again, this was a meeting about an exhibition at Ambrose's little place up the hill. He and my mother had a bit of an argy-bargy over who should be included in the show. It was nothing serious – you can take my word for that. I know when she's really angry or upset. Her eyes bulge. But she kept pointing out that his desire for a Cassatt was simply out of range. And he kept insisting that he had enough connections, especially through the master, to get hold of some real master-pieces by women. I got the feeling . . .'

'Yes?' prompted St. Just.

'I got the feeling he felt a bit put down by my mother. Not an uncommon occurrence. She can be rather . . . oh, how to put it? A bit strong-minded. A bit of a know-it-all.' She paused, then added, 'More than a bit.'

'So,' said St. Just. 'Do you plan to live here permanently with her? In this house?'

'Absolutely not!' She hunched her shoulders in a shudder of horror. 'Not if I can help it. I've been looking at rentals, each one further from town than the last. The bus ride and so on, the parking fees, make it not worth the move. And I'd have to have a flatmate, which brings its own terrors. But yes, I will have to get out of here soon. Like I said, I want my own life. And my mother has rather firm ideas about how I should live it.'

'I see. And of course, how you spend your time is your business.'

'Precisely.'

'And with whom.'

'Quite.'

'Does she approve of Rufus?'

'I don't know. She should. He's—'

'A genius. We know. Now, as to when the party broke up. What time was that?'

'I've been trying to remember, actually,' she said. 'There was quite a bit of drinking. People lingered – you know. But I'm quite sure that they left well before midnight. I stayed here, of course, and did the washing-up. And then I went to bed and was fast asleep before my head hit the pillow. A little too much wine. I didn't hear anything about the master until rather late the next day. My mother got a phone call from the college. One of her colleagues. You know, the grapevine was going full tilt.'

'Did you know the master at all?'

'No more than any other student. I was there so briefly.' She shrugged. 'He seemed nice enough. One of these very distinguished-looking people. And clearly born to be an academic.'

'In what way?'

'A bit head in the clouds, you know. Maybe it's something to do with always having your mind in a different century. They're all like that, these dons.'

'Your mother included?' This was from Sergeant Fear. Again, he didn't normally intervene in interviews, so there was generally a point to his interventions.

'Not really. She's very much of the moment, my mother. Her moment.'

St. Just asked, 'So, the dinner broke up around . . . when again?'

'I didn't say, and I can't be sure, but it was maybe eleven thirty. I do remember it was late for us. We usually have something at seven, and sometimes it's just me. My mother has a lot of female friends, and they like to gather at all the restaurants. Me, I've had enough restaurants for the day by the time I get home.'

'Your shift at the restaurant is early then?'

'Yes, for now. You have to work your way up to the big dinner rush. The pay is better and of course, you learn to handle the pressure-cooker atmosphere of a restaurant kitchen.'

'And you didn't accompany Rufus Penn back to the college? Your boyfriend?'

'No, we'd been seeing quite a bit of each other, and needed a break. I was tired and he had something or other planned for the next day. It will be different when we're able to be together in New York and he's not so preoccupied with his studies.'

St. Just wondered how much Rufus knew of her thinking. As to the rest, it was a reasonable response, but it didn't ring true.

'You didn't perhaps meet him over there later?'

'Why in the world would I? If you don't believe me, why don't you check the college security cameras? They would show me walking in if I'd been there. Which I was not. The gates are locked at midnight, so someone would have had to let me in. And the rules are no visitors after midnight.'

'Rules are made to be broken.'

'But as I've already told you,' she said with a heavy sigh of exasperation, 'I went to bed. I was asleep almost immediately. I was tired after a day at the restaurant and then cooking here at home. I'd drunk a lot of red wine. I slept like a rock.'

'Lucky you. There comes a day when wine interferes with sleep and I'm afraid I've nearly reached that day,' said St. Just. He stood, followed by Sergeant Fear. 'Well, thank you for your time. If there are any further questions, what would be the best way to reach you during the day?'

'I have to leave for the restaurant in about an hour to help set up. I'm filling in for someone who called in sick.'

'Thank you very much for your time.'

She nodded, suddenly glum. 'I hope you get him – whoever did this. Sir Flyte was not a person who made many enemies, I would have said.'

'And yet, apparently, he made at least one. And one is all it takes.'

THIRTEEN
Mother of the Year

After the two policemen left the Peyton interview, they stood quietly taking in the front garden, first making sure the door had closed firmly behind them.

Peyton had said nothing to raise alarms, but St. Just was dissatisfied just the same.

'Rufus certainly has her in thrall,' he said.

Sergeant Fear nodded. 'It looks like someone's been gardening,' he said. 'Deadheading the roses. The soil's all disturbed.'

'I keep meaning to do that. No time, of course. Portia's taken over and says she enjoys it, but I need to pitch in and help.'

Heads down and hands clasped behind their backs, they walked slowly towards the car.

'Where to next?' asked Sergeant Fear.

'I guess we talk to the mother. Peyton's mother. Just to cross all the T's and dot the I's.'

'Surely uniform will be on that?'

'They will get round to her eventually. I don't want to use them for anything right now other than interviewing the possible witnesses at the college, before they leave for their classes and whatnot. And the witnesses must be legion. It is going to take a huge amount of manpower to sift through all the reports and follow up on the more promising accounts.'

'There were plenty of people standing around, weren't there?'

'After the fact, of course. But any kind of disturbance in that rather sanctified place would arouse curiosity. Especially among those in Second Court, the nearest to First. I don't know about Third Court. It might be worth doing a little sound test to see exactly how far a cry from the Master's Lodge

would travel at midnight – without the usual daytime inter-
ference, but with the complication of those bells going off.
Has anyone verified the bells are accurate?'

'I'll look into it.'

'Anyway, look up the mother's office for us, and we'll see
if we can find her in there. I believe women's studies are held
in the Atroni Building.'

The Atroni was one of the modern buildings that architects
had managed to wedge into the footprint of Cambridge, struc-
tures that tried either to blend in or stand out, but to St. Just's
eyes failed abysmally at both.

He was a traditionalist, like King Charles. He couldn't see
any improvement in inserting glass and steel where they didn't
belong, not in a grand old town like Cambridge, which to his
mind would have been improved by being left alone. It only
needed the occasional shoring up when brick and stone began
to crumble and fall into the River Cam.

An old rhyme came to mind, no doubt prompted by his
recent visit to Hardwick College: 'Hardwick Hall, more glass
than wall.' He must remember to ask someone what – if any
– connection the college had to the infamous, enormously
wealthy Bess of Hardwick.

Sergeant Fear's reaction was different. As they pulled up in
front of the offices of the Department of Women's Studies, he
let out a gasp of admiration.

'I've never been in this part of town since they built this,'
he said. 'I think they did a good job, don't you?'

The inarticulate grunt in reply was all the answer he needed.
St. Just didn't seem to realize that progress was progress and
allowances had to be made for the increasing influx into the
city of students – and the people needed to support them. Not
to mention the tourists who brought much-needed revenue
each summer.

Who would want to go back to medieval days, anyway? No
running water, no electricity? Everyone smelling like they'd
slept with the livestock, which often they had? No telly? They
could keep it.

St. Just pulled the car into a space reserved for faculty. He put a card on the dash bearing the emblem of the Cambridgeshire Constabulary – a crowned Brunswick star – which stated they were there on police business. There was a number to call if anyone felt like complaining about it, but any amount of complaining wouldn't move the car until he and Fear were ready to leave.

The Department of Women's Studies was announced by a prominent sign out front. It did not have an emblem – a circle above a cross might have been suitable at one time – but he imagined committee meetings on the topic would be fraught. On the third floor down a wide hallway, they found the offices of Professor Patricia Beadle-Batsford.

Sergeant Fear had called ahead, and she was waiting for them – her hands folded tightly on her desk, one thumb massaging the knuckle of the other. The professor of women's studies was a thin woman of middling years who wore her thick brown hair in an unfortunate Prince Valiant haircut.

She had deep-set dark eyes that needed no make-up and strong brows that could have done with a trim. She wore a blue blazer and brown scarf that picked up the colour of her eyes. Her only adornment was a heavy gold chain that held the scarf in place. No rings on her fingers, and – St. Just assumed – no bells on her toes.

She didn't look pleased to see them. She struggled to find a suitable expression, finally settling on distaste.

The office itself was functional, clean, and spare as a monk's cell. The only signs of personalization were a white vase of flowers on the windowsill. Someone had been to the Saturday market. He recognized the same mixed arrangement from the vendor where he often bought flowers for Portia. At this time of year, yellow and orange chrysanthemums and red berries predominated.

St. Just looked closely at Professor Beadle-Batsford, thinking she seemed armed for a war of words. A police presence wasn't welcome for many but rather something to be endured, like a visit to the dentist.

Someone had put her back up, however. Perhaps her daughter had given her a ring. Or the curator. Her first words confirmed this impression.

'I don't have the least idea why you're wasting my time with this. I held a dinner party and that is the extent of my involvement.'

'May I remind you a man is dead, Professor.'

'Yes, yes, of course, and it's terrible. Terrible what happened to the master. Shocking. A perfect example of male aggression and testosterone-fuelled anger run amok. It will be a period of great upheaval, and finding a replacement for Flyte will take time. That said, of course, it's past time for a woman to take the helm. I shall certainly be putting forward several names.'

'Including your own?' asked St. Just, with an innocent bat of his eyes.

He was fighting back the instinct to dislike the woman practically on sight, but of all the things to be concerned about, the election of a new college master seemed like the least of anyone's worries. Although he'd been prepared for this reaction, it still came as a bit of a shock.

But then, the college had probably survived worse over the long centuries.

'I refuse to apologize for my ambition,' she said hotly, perhaps picking up on his judgement. 'Or to be shamed for it. It's always the same old story: ambition in a woman means she's some kind of shrew or vixen or worse. Ambition in a man means he's a genius destined for high office and best of luck to him.'

'I didn't mean to imply—'

'This is why it is past time Hardwick College – which carries the name of a strong, indomitable, and clever woman after all – should finally emerge into the twenty-first century, shaking off the shackles of history and embracing the future unafraid.'

St. Just had heard enough. 'Do you think you would be able to revisit the night of the tragedy and tell us if the master's name came up in conversation at your dinner party?'

She spluttered to a halt, clearly not expecting the question. 'Whyever should his name have come up?'

'Because I understand he is one of the leading experts on art history and you were planning an exhibition of women's art. It seems evident why his name would come up.'

Sergeant Fear hazarded a glance at St. Just. He was generally much gentler with female witnesses, but he seemed to be going in for the kill here quite quickly.

'I'll go further,' continued St. Just. 'I should think that not including him in the planning for this exhibition would be an obvious slight, amounting to an insult to his expertise and his authority at the college. Are you expecting us to believe he wasn't consulted?'

'He wasn't consulted for the simple reason he didn't regard women's art as worth the wood it was painted on, or the clay it was moulded from. I couldn't be bothered to consult him.'

'I see,' said St. Just. He had not in fact anticipated this, and he felt he should have. Was she telling the truth? Had the master been a known misogynist with a blind eye when it came to women in the arts?

St. Just was kicking himself. It was a basic rule of interrogation that you should never ask a question unless you could anticipate the answer.

'Was this perhaps an opinion of yours, or can you better explain why he would be left out of such an important discussion? A man, after all, at the head of your own college. Was there some, erm, *history* there between you two? No pun intended, but he was an authority on the history of art, which would include women artists. Perhaps this had caused a clash between you in the past?'

'No.'

'No what?'

'There was no clash. And I resent this heavy-handed attempt to drag me into a situation in which I clearly had no part. I believe I should be contacting my solicitor. You can talk to her.'

'We'd be delighted, but of course there's no suggestion you'll be taken in for questioning.'

'They said the same thing to the suffragettes. And all those poor women wanted was the vote. For their trouble they were beaten and starved in British prisons by men such as yourself.'

It was costing St. Just a great deal of effort to hang on to his temper. He could feel his blood pressure start to rise.

'That is an absurd and slanderous accusation and a ridiculous parallel to draw. We are conducting a murder inquiry and, Professor Beadle-Batsford, any lack of cooperation on your part will certainly be noted, reported, and no doubt acted upon.'

Sergeant Fear, taking his cue, began scribbling furiously.

'This is outrageous. By whom would it be acted upon?'

'By the vice chancellor of the university, of course,' said St. Just. 'That's whom.'

This was an enormous stretch but, once the words had left his mouth, he realized that would be the only recourse open to him.

The woman was the head of her department, and it would take a lot to inveigle a higher authority to intervene. At the same time he knew that the vice chancellor, Lady Felicity Griffiths – he had met her during an awards ceremony for the constabulary – would do anything to avoid any suggestion that an already scandalous situation involving the murder of a master might be fuelled by a lack of cooperation from a Cambridge professor, however tangentially that professor might be involved in the situation.

To his astonishment this wild threat, born of desperation, seemed to do the trick. Her imagination likely had created a video showing how this might play out in front of Lady Felicity – who was no doubt someone in whose good graces she needed to remain. Especially if she fancied her chances of being elected master of Hardwick College.

'Very well,' she said with ill grace. 'What is it you want to know?'

'You can start by telling us why you organized the party.'

'Why I organized the party? Isn't it obvious? So that we could talk over an important matter, but in a relaxed atmosphere. I don't like meeting in coffee shops, which has become the default, and this was not anything I wanted to discuss in a crowded restaurant. It just seemed like the nice thing – the correct thing – to do.'

'And your daughter being there? I mean, did she have a lot to contribute?'

'You've spoken with my daughter?'

'We just came from your house.'

'I think you might have mentioned interrogating my daughter before now. Is this some kind of trap?'

'I'm not going to dignify that with an answer. We're talking to everyone tangentially or directly connected with the events of that night.'

'Well, it's hardly my fault, is it, that Ambrose Nussknacker was at my dinner party after meeting with the master. Surely it would make more sense to talk to Mr Nussknacker.'

'What a good idea,' said St. Just. 'But it was a very small party, including your daughter, and including an art history graduate student. It just seems rather lopsided to me.'

She seemed to acknowledge his point. She sighed and said, 'My daughter insisted on inviting him, if you must know.'

'Him being Rufus Penn?'

'Yes. She's rather taken with him, I'm afraid, and we were looking to even out the numbers with a male–female seating.'

'How very traditional.'

She paused, perhaps to tweak her rules of dining etiquette to accommodate her sense of feminist outrage.

'I suppose,' she said, 'some traditions linger, in spite of our best efforts to free ourselves from those chains.'

'Yes, quite. You didn't approve of Rufus Penn, I take it?'

'I'd rather not question my daughter's judgement.'

'Very wise, I'm sure. Young people so seldom take good advice, anyway. Whose idea was this exhibition?'

'It was the curator's idea, initially. The exhibition is meant to showcase a blend of classic and contemporary pieces that challenge the art world's male-centric dominance throughout the centuries. There are galleries in the world that still don't have a single woman artist represented.'

'And when would this exhibition you're organizing open?'

'It's still in the early planning stages. But recent events have certainly cast a shadow over the timeline.'

'Why do you say that?'

'Um. Well . . .'

'Yes?'

'Well, if you must know, we were planning to ask the master to write an introduction to the catalogue. There was no getting around the fact that he had a great deal of clout in the art world, even though his views were one-sided and misogynistic to the point of savagery. The curator felt that could be overcome. I had my doubts. Ambrose seemed to feel he was making headway, however.'

'Is that what Ambrose talked about with the master earlier in the day?'

'I've no idea what they talked about.'

'Did Rufus Penn have much to contribute to this conversation?'

'No,' she said. 'For once, he was rather quiet and respectful.'

'I see. Do you know him well?'

Suddenly, she would not meet his eyes.

'Well, do you?'

'It was a second meeting. The first time, I found him rather full of himself. But he was there to learn, it seemed, that evening. And perhaps to admit the possibility the world didn't always revolve around him, despite his looks. Plus, I think he was enjoying his food. The meals in Hall are not everything a young man used to the best might desire.'

'He was used to the best?'

'You don't recognize the name?'

'I'm afraid I don't.'

'If you lived in America, you would. He comes from a long line of gilded-age robber barons, from back in the days before the rich were forced to pay taxes. They accumulated quite a fortune and, unlike the Vanderbilts, have managed not to squander it all. Penn. That name must mean something to you.'

'Apart from Pennsylvania, I can't say that it does.' Still, he felt they had wandered a bit from the topic. He didn't see how Rufus Penn's family wealth had much to do with anything, but it did explain his sense of entitlement.

'Tell me when the dinner party broke up.'

'What time did my daughter tell you?'

'I'm asking you.'

She hesitated, her eyes not on him but boring into her desk. She resumed the rather vicious massaging of her thumb knuckle. 'I can't say I paid close attention. The party went on for some time.'

'Take a guess,' said St. Just. 'We won't hold you to it.'

'Before midnight. Now, do let me know if there's something else you need. If not, I really must—'

'Who left the party and in what order?'

'The two men left together,' she answered quickly. They had reached a question she could safely answer.

'They left in the same car?'

'I assume,' she said. 'I didn't stand in the front garden and wave them off as if they were going to war, but I believe that was their intent. Ambrose said he would drop Rufus off at the college and then continue home.'

'And you were left at home with your daughter?'

'Yes.'

'Who did the washing-up?'

'We did. We did the washing-up together.'

'Did you stay up or go immediately to bed?'

'We went to bed immediately after.'

'And how did you hear about the master?'

'Yesterday morning. I got a call from the bursar. He was quite distraught, poor man.'

'They were close?'

'They were friendly.' She paused, considering. 'But I think it's more that this creates a situation. A situation, and a bit of atmosphere, the bursar would rather not have to deal with. The loss of a master of a college is a tear in the fabric, you know. And the election of a new master is not without its dangers. The politics of the thing. It doesn't bear thinking about. I think the bursar was hoping I'd, you know, pitch in to help. Of course, I told him I'd be hap—'

'Well.' St. Just slapped his knees preparatory to standing. She was returning to her not-too-subtle plans to lead the college. 'I think we've taken enough of your time.'

She nodded. 'I should rather think you have.'

'Enjoy your day,' he said.

'In a fairer world, I would.'

As the men walked down granite stairs to the ground floor, Sergeant Fear could not contain himself.

'The daughter said she did the washing-up. She didn't say it was a joint effort.'

'I caught that, too. A definite contradiction there. I hope you made a note of it.'

Sergeant Fear patted his jacket pocket. 'It's all right here. I feel she had a nerve, don't you, sir? I mean, really. What did all that about the suffragettes have to do with anything?'

'Yes. It makes me wonder, her extreme reaction.'

'Wonder what?'

'Who she's protecting. Sorry, *whom*. I'll give you three guesses.'

FOURTEEN
Speak No Evil

Zola Blaze, the day porter at Hardwick College, had left her child at the Tiny Bundles Day Nursery, but not without a fight. Since she and Derek had split up, the problem was not childcare but perhaps too much childcare.

In other words, his sudden interest in Lucille was designed to impress the courts and play the system, not to impress or help Zola or their child. Zola felt she was seeing through Derek for the first time, as if he were made of glass.

Around Lucille, Zola had to be careful not to use any of the names she privately called him, in case Lucille could understand her mutterings. The kid was smart and didn't miss much.

But suddenly, the simple act of dropping her child off in the mornings teemed with drama, which she feared was going to be the source of many sessions with a psychiatrist in Lucille's future.

The game Derek was playing was to make her late for work and ultimately to get her fired, so he could claim she was not fit to raise a child and completely unable to do so without a salary. Zola had her army pension but it wasn't enough; with a child, another source of income was necessary.

She had wondered more than once how in the world she had ended up married to such a perfectly evil, spiteful man. What was in her own childhood that would make her that desperate? She supposed it was some form of PTSD from her time in the army. God only knew.

What looked on the surface like a happy-go-lucky persona was, in Derek's case, a nearly criminal lack of responsibility, making his quarrels and insistence on custody all the more absurd. She wondered if she should pretend indifference: tell him he could keep the child, claiming she was far too much trouble, too hard to take care of, too demanding. But not for a minute could she give Derek that opening. Reverse psychology didn't always work, and the courts and the social workers assigned to their case would be watching carefully for signs of her being the unfit mother Derek was claiming.

She wouldn't have worried so much about the situation except that her ex was a solicitor. One of the slippery brands of solicitor, the kind who would concoct evidence if needs be to win a case. And he nearly always won. His strategy during the divorce had been to bury her in paperwork, threaten her job, besmirch her reputation – a game of psychological warfare that was as effective as it was detestable.

In her heart, she knew he did not really want Lucille; he simply could not bear to lose to Zola. His ego would not allow it.

She managed to find a parking space; by her watch, she was now exactly two minutes late. Fortunately, Oliver, the night porter, was aware of her situation – she had talked about it often enough – and he was happy to make allowances. She never wanted to take advantage of his kindness, however. The man had his own problems.

The porter's job was not one she took lightly. Oliver had the easier part of it; there was very little that required his attention at night. During the daytime, though, especially during term, the post was extremely busy. The students were a joy and a nuisance all at once. Sometimes Zola felt Lucille was better prepared for life than some of them.

She finished putting on her uniform in the car, an innovation to her routine that added five extra minutes to her morning and allowed her to get Lucille to Tiny Bundles early enough to miss Derek, though he would soon catch on to this ploy.

She pulled her black jacket over her white shirt, straightened her tie, and changed from her driving moccasins into her practical, highly polished black shoes. It was basically a male uniform adopted for the female form – and badly, at that. No one had hips this wide outside of a zoo.

But this was Oxbridge, and the sight of a porter wearing a well-fitted dress would probably set them back centuries, unsplitting the atom.

She wore her hair short, for the arrival of Lucille had meant streamlining her personal care routine. Besides, with Derek out of her life, she wasn't particularly interested in doing much more than make sure she was clean and presentable. Things like dating apps were for other people – people with a higher tolerance for risk than she had, at that.

As far as Zola was concerned, it was Zola and her daughter against the world. She would worry about dating when Lucille was safely in college – maybe even here at Hardwick. Any kid who could build a house out of blocks at age three clearly had a bright future ahead of her.

Of course, her thoughts flew to Lucille when Oliver told her about the events surrounding the murder of the master. Was the job even safe? He'd told her about the scream, about searching the lodge and finally finding the body, all the while playing down his fear and playing up his masterful command of the situation.

She didn't call him on it, of course. The poor guy had thought, like her, that as a porter he was escaping all the shattering events of his life.

And yet here they both were in the thick of things.

She knew Oliver struggled at times to keep up with the job, and she was faced with the dilemma of reporting him or not. If this was some kind of mad crime scene, with a serial killer at large, surely it was her job to tell the authorities so they could put in someone more alert. Or give Oliver backup to make sure the place was guarded at night.

The problem was, with the master dead, no one was really in charge. She supposed the dean or the bursar would be the people to talk to, but she couldn't bring herself to rat on Oliver for anything, let alone for keeping his own counsel. And surely they'd never have the budget to hire extra security.

Keeping one's own counsel. Quite sensible when she thought about it.

She kept hoping that everything would die down quickly, and she'd be able, in good conscience, to let the man ease into a slow and dignified retirement.

Everything looked as usual as she headed for the Porters' Lodge, until her steps from the car park took her past the

Master's Lodge, still barricaded and defiled with crime scene
tape. What in the name of God was going on, that crime scene
tape should mar this stodgy old mausoleum she had come to
love?

It was her place of refuge. The master being murdered had
no place in her life.

Oliver wasn't on duty at the desk, but that wasn't unexpected.
Sometimes in the mornings she found him asleep in front of
the telly, BBC Breakfast blaring away. Sometimes they
watched the show together for a few moments, if something
interesting was going on in the world.

The door to the porters' sitting room wasn't completely
shut.

This never happened. There was access from the gatehouse,
of course, for the students to get to their pigeonholes, but the
door into the Porters' Lodge proper was always closed.

It was not so much a security measure as an off-limits notice
to the students who might want to wander in to whinge about
something or other. That new American chap in particular
seemed to regard the porters as a special breed of high-end
waiter sent to do his bidding, with no higher purpose in life
than to see to his happiness. They'd soon freeze that off him,
but it would be a long few months for all concerned in the
meanwhile.

The door's standing ajar was unusual, but perhaps Oliver
had nipped away to use the gents'. She inched it further open,
not expecting to see anything out of the ordinary. She could
hear the telly, the announcer solemnly announcing another
flare-up in the world.

She slid off her backpack, nudging the door wider, her mind
still on Lucille and Derek. She often wondered how far she
would go to get her child away from him. Move to Marrakech
or somewhere like that, change her name and appearance? Did
she really think Lucille was in danger from her father? Or was
it simply that his values were so utterly opposed to Zola's
own?

She began sorting things from her backpack. The lunch she
had packed for herself – cheese and tomato and lettuce on
wholewheat bread, an apple and – to offset the wholesomeness

of all that – a chocolate hazelnut bar. She had a flask full of coffee and some bottled water in an ecologically friendly container. She slid all this into the bottom drawer of the public-facing desk, from behind which the porters dealt with visitors and their massively important problems.

Most often it would be a student who had misplaced their keys. Once in a great while, a *very* great while, something had gone missing from their rooms. But in this environment, theft was rare. Often a mobile phone gone missing and believed stolen had simply been left in the pub after one too many pints and without the 'Find My Phone' option switched on.

The master's death, of course, had upended the college's nearly blemish-free safety record.

'Oliver,' she called loudly over her shoulder, hoping to wake him from his slumber so he'd not be caught asleep at the wheel. She got no response, so she repeated the call. Perhaps he couldn't hear with the telly on.

Unknowingly, she was mimicking the events of the night Oliver had found the master dead.

Having tucked the empty backpack in the kneehole of the desk, she entered the Porters' Lodge, the area with the chair and TV and Oliver's bits of sports paraphernalia scattered about.

Later, she would think it was a mercy for her he hadn't been stabbed; she didn't think she could cope with that. She found him with a gunshot wound to the head, perhaps a mercy for him. It would've been quick. It was nothing she hadn't seen before, but of course, this was Oliver. Sweet, dear, harmless Oliver.

She had a crazy thought that it must be a joke, that he was trying to scare her, but she knew perfectly well that practical jokes had never been his style. He was too kind for that.

She felt his wrist for a pulse, then went to dial 999 on her mobile.

She had remembered the unusual name of the detective, and instructed the responder to notify DCI St. Just immediately. The woman at the call centre did not take this well, being told her job, and said she'd 'get someone out, never you mind who'. But when Zola explained her location and the urgency of her business, there was no further arguing.

'Hardwick College. There's been another murder,' she'd said, scarcely believing her own ears.

Zola imagined the word had spread like wildfire through the police ranks that the master had been murdered.

And now – clearly – the night porter. It might've been staged as a suicide, but she knew it for what it was. She even recognized the type of gun lying on the floor – a World War II trophy, probably brought home from Germany.

No question, the thing still worked, even after more than eighty years. That much was evident.

Someone had been taking good care of it.

St. Just was just prepping the coffee pot with a filter and the special Free Trade grind, portioning it out like so much gold dust.

Portia was still asleep at this hour, just after six a.m. She'd told him she didn't have a supervision until ten, and a lecture at one.

She would be writing her newest crime novel in between. He was never sure how she managed to flip from one thing to the other, but she assured him it was all kind of the same thing in her mind: criminology classes and writing about crime. A ceaseless back and forth, ebb and flow, evidence and suspects and sociology and police methods.

He knew there were many other demands on her time, for her students adored her. Everyone wanted to be guided by the best and recommended by a known expert in the field. Both male and female students equally saw her haloed attraction.

The phone rang, and he picked it up quickly before it could wake her. He listened intently, asking only, 'When?'

Then he switched off the coffee pot and left behind a note for Portia.

He and Sergeant Fear arrived in record time at Hardwick College, this time parking before the gate, tossing the 'police business' card on the dashboard.

They passed through the iron-studded wooden doors beneath the college's coat of arms, carved into the stone archway. The simple design, lacking the usual spears and weapons, now seemed especially at odds with the college's bloody history.

One of Hardwick College's brushes with serious wrongdoing had been an eighteenth-century crime of passion involving a middle-aged bedder and a choirmaster or doctor of divinity – accounts varied.

In the nineteenth century, a scholar had accused a college servant named Ralph Leatherwood of stealing a neckerchief. The scholar had killed him, claiming to have caught Ralph red-handed.

There had been conflicting accounts: Ralph had been killed by being strangled with the neckerchief, by being dropped out of a window headfirst onto the pavement below, or by being forced to swallow cyanide. There was evidence the story was true in one of its forms, for there was a stone bench in Third Court with a plaque that read Ralph (Servant), RIP.

Zola wondered why no one could be troubled to inscribe Ralph's full name but his murder was mentioned in the college digitized archives, which she had spent many happy hours perusing. The unnamed murderer, the son of a viscount, had been sent down, presumably to advance his career of crime in London.

And now here was Oliver, another faithful servant, with a bullet hole in his head and a gun on the floor by his side. The suggestion to be drawn was that he had killed himself out of grief at having killed the master, perhaps in a fit of rage over some perceived slight.

But Zola had read far too many detective stories to fall for that simple solution, however elegantly it would tie up the case.

For one thing, she knew Oliver too well. He didn't have fits of rage and he held nothing whatsoever against the master. Moreover, he would never bring that disgrace on his grandson, who walked on water in Oliver's eyes. Who *needed* him, in Oliver's eyes.

And for yet another thing, she knew what the killer clearly did not: Oliver was left-handed, but the gun lay neatly on the floor at his right side.

No left-handed person ever tried to kill themselves with their right hand. Twenty years with the military police had much to teach those who knew how to keep their eyes open. Zola had seen more suicides in the military than she had ever thought possible.

The scene was set, but Oliver's death couldn't have happened the way the killer wanted the police to believe.

'Is that what I think it is?' asked St. Just.

'If you mean a Luger, yes,' said Dr Pomeroy, adjusting his glasses with a sigh. 'Vintage. The real item.'

'Not the best weapon if you're trying not to be heard, though. There's no suppressor on it.'

'No. One can be fitted to an antique like this, but it would be a bit fiddly.'

'An antique,' St. Just repeated. 'From World War Two. Amazing to think that era is receding into history. What's the falling-off point? I suppose when the last person with direct memory of events passes on. Anyway, it's not a common weapon these days.'

'Perhaps not openly on display in people's houses, if that is what you mean. But these old guns are still around more than we would care to think. Many soldiers came back from the European theatre with souvenirs: undeclared, unremarked and, needless to say, unregistered in most cases, since they were obtained illegally, often taken off the bodies of the dead. The P08 nine-millimetre Parabellum – *para bellum,* or "prepare for war" – was known for its accuracy but mostly coveted for its design.'

'Prepare for war,' St. Just murmured. Looking at the slumped-over figure of the porter, he said, 'Poor old fellow. I'm sure he knew all about that. It didn't help him in the end.'

'It's true that I don't see many of these in my day-to-day job,' said Dr Pomeroy. 'And if I'm honest, I haven't seen any used as a weapon in the commission of a crime. After all, why bother with an outmoded weapon that might misfire when the streets are alive with modern guns, ghost guns, guns assembled from online sites? All you need is a Tor browser nowadays, and you're in business.'

'And a terrible business it is. Anyway, the shot was at close range to the right temple. Even I can see that. Death was instantaneous, I hope?'

'Yes. Going with the evidence of my eyes I would call it suicide, but the day porter who found him – her name is Zola Blaze – says he was not right-handed. She is adamant about that.'

'Not right-handed,' St. Just repeated quietly.

'And truly, I would say with one hundred per cent certainty, if you are determined to end your life, you're not going to risk surviving with a horrible disfigurement or disability for life.'

'Right. You are going to use your strongest hand to aim straight and get it over with.'

'We will need to investigate his background,' Pomeroy continued, 'to see if he had anything going on in his life that would warrant ending it. An autopsy will show us evidence of any disease that might make choosing instantaneous death more attractive than a lingering death.'

'I'll need a word with the day porter. Zola, is it? Where is she?'

'You'll find her in the senior common room. Exceptions were made. Normally, students and staff alike are not allowed in there outside of special occasions, apart from the cleaning staff, of course.'

'I would call murder a special occasion, wouldn't you?' St. Just paused, looking around him at the comfortable room where Oliver had spent so many hours. 'I don't know a great deal about Lugers. How loud would a shot have been? Loud enough to be heard beyond First Court?'

'Under normal circumstances, yes, and loud enough to be heard by passers-by in the street. I'll examine the gun to see if it's been adapted to deaden the sound, but if it was—'

'The killer stayed to remove the suppressor.'

'Right. But it was probably the dead of night. The porter's been dead three to eight hours – I'll know more later, of course. The killer may just have been making doubly certain he wouldn't be raising the alarm with a loud noise, but perhaps no one was around to hear, anyway.'

'The outer gate is meant to be closed at midnight to outsiders. I'm sure Oliver learned his lesson after the master was killed. That might help us establish time of death. Say, between the time he came on duty at ten and before he locked up at midnight.'

'I have to go by the science rather than supposing what lessons the porter may or may not have learned,' said Pomeroy, 'but those times are certainly within the range.'

'If a suppressor is the answer, that means finding an armourer or mechanic with that sort of skill. This area is stiff with history-and-gun aficionados, hunters, and so on. It probably would not be hard to come up with a list of a dozen such experts who might remember or have kept records of adapting a gun of that ilk and that era.

'But would they own up to it?' St. Just continued. 'Would they have kept records? Would they even still be alive? I think the latter is the relevant question.'

'Yes, we're talking about a different century now,' said the pathologist.

'Anyway, suppressors . . . Are they strictly for the bad guys? A suppressor doesn't necessarily mean wanting to murder someone quietly.'

'No. The argument is they reduce recoil and muzzle blast.' Dr Pomeroy, having finished his initial inspection, began putting the tools of his trade away in his black case.

'I'll get Henderson on it. He's a gun enthusiast.' St. Just had little interest in guns. He knew how to handle one, but it was not part of his arsenal, so to speak. He would on occasion do target practice, not because it was fun, but because knowing how to shoot might one day be required of him. With more weapons on the street, he could no longer rule it out as a possibility. 'Worst day of Henderson's life was when they banned fox hunting,' he added.

'I'm sorry?'

'I mean to say he is into every possible outdoor sport – trail hunting, fishing, white-water rafting, tree climbing – you name it. So Henderson is likely to know the expert we're looking for. When can we get a better estimate of the time of death?'

'I'll aim for later today, but there was a shooting in the city yesterday afternoon. Not far from where we're standing, in fact. Initially, no one was thought to be killed, but now I'm told it was a domestic incident and the victim did not survive. The chief is out of his mind with what looks like a major breakdown in civilization in our little patch. I've been instructed to prioritize that incident. Of course, that was before the porter was found.'

St. Just took another look round. 'It's a small room. If someone was looking for something, it wouldn't take long to search in here. We'll need someone to see if anything looks out of place. Probably Zola, once the body's been removed.'

'Right.'

'I'll have a word with the chief,' said St. Just. 'After all, I have two murders to solve, and I don't imagine a shooting in broad daylight, no doubt with witnesses, requires your fullest attention as to cause of death.'

'Agreed. And the longer this madman is loose at Hardwick College, the harder my job is going to get.'

'A madman? Do you really think that's the case?'

'It was a figure of speech. Whoever did this is brazen, but I don't think crazed. There's a method here, a precision. Wouldn't you say?'

'I would. I'll speak with the dean and let him know the college won't be able to carry on quite as before. They're all used to holding online lectures and supervisions by now, anyway.'

FIFTEEN
Best Not Speak of It

St. Just found Zola Blaze coiled in a plush chair in the senior common room, cradling a cuppa given to her by the bedder in charge of cleaning the space sacred to the college dons. The day porter looked composed, but there was no hiding the blankness in her eyes and the woodenness of her movements that spoke of shock. It was an impression underlined by her first words.

'I don't know how I'll explain this to my daughter,' she said softly. 'She was crazy about Oliver and he about her. She's young now so I can say Ollie was sorry but he had to go away, but even when she's older, she won't understand this.' She looked up at St. Just, then away. 'What adults do to each other – how in the world do you explain that to a little girl?'

'I have no idea, Ms Blaze.' He took the chair opposite. 'Let's start by catching whoever did it, shall we? The best way we can do that quickly is if you can tell me everything you know that was going on in Oliver Staunton's life.'

'He wasn't suicidal,' she said stoutly. 'Let's start there. He was a man of the most . . . *stalwart* nature.' She had to reach for the word, but then nodded to herself, as if she found it fitted her needs perfectly. '*Stalwart*. He endured. He was getting old, yes, some people thought he was past it, yes, but he was a brave man, and I won't have it said he committed suicide when I know there is no way he would do that. Not to his grandson. The grandson was all he had left. He wouldn't do this to . . . to that . . . to him.'

She ended the sentence in a strangled voice, fumbling in her pocket for a tissue to wipe the tears now threatening to overflow. Finding none, she brushed her eyes with her jacket sleeve as St. Just handed her a packet of tissues. He always carried them in his pocket for moments like this.

'Thanks,' she said briefly. 'I swore I wouldn't do this – cry or break down. And this is awful to even have come into my mind, but I'm thinking my ex will get wind of it – of course he will, from the news – and try to twist it somehow to fit his "unfit mother" narrative.' She cleared her throat. 'What is it you need to know?'

'You can begin by telling me why, apart from knowing his character, you feel so strongly Oliver had so much to live for.'

'There was Gerry, the grandson. Well . . . this is awkward – difficult for me to say because Oliver trusted me to keep my mouth shut, but . . . Oliver loved him, that's all. There's no explaining these things. I met Gerry once, and I would've said there was no mastermind at work there. And no sporting skills or mathematical ability or simple kindness or anything that would point up Gerry as one of God's great inventions.

'But as a mother myself, I know full well that everything my daughter does makes me think she's a prodigy.' She tried for a self-mocking smile that dislodged another tear. Fiercely, she wiped it away. 'And that's how Oliver regarded Gerry. But Gerry had reached an age where keeping in touch with his grandfather wasn't a priority. He didn't seem to care. And if I'm going to be honest, which I must be to help you, I think there was a bit of drug use there. And him with kids and all.'

'Dealing?'

'I couldn't say, but using. Yeah, for sure. So many broken dates with his grandfather – they would arrange to meet for coffee or something, and the kid just wouldn't show up, no explanation, no apology. At best, he'd claim to have lost his phone. If he did bother to show up to some fancy restaurant Oliver could barely afford, it was to ask for money. I know it broke Oliver's heart.'

'You know this, how?'

'Because he told me. Like I said, he trusted me and now, here I am, nattering away . . . Anyway, the very fact I became a confidante tells you the extent of his hurt because, believe me, this was a man who kept everything to himself. But talking to a single mother going through a hellish divorce was an easier fit for Oliver than telling his troubles to his mates down the pub. You know, for them he'd do the stiff upper lip, macho thing. Probably lie or imply Gerry was constantly in touch. It broke my heart, and I knew without having to be told it broke Oliver's as well. Oh, but I don't mean . . . No, it wouldn't drive him to . . . damn Gerry, anyway. What does a simple effing phone call cost anyone?'

He looked at her a long minute, watching for the moment she returned to herself. It might be fleeting. At last he said, 'I am dreadfully sorry to have to do this now, but we've never spoken before and it's urgent now that we do. That may have been an oversight on the part of the police. We're spread rather thin, you see.'

'I was wondering when someone would interview me,' she said.

He sat back in the worn leather chair. 'Are you saying you have some information that could throw light on what happened to Mr Staunton or the master?'

She shook her head. 'If I had anything straightforward to tell you, anything that was clear in my own mind, I would've come to you right away – confidence or no confidence. But I wasn't sure, you see, and other people were involved. Not to mention the good name of the college. I just couldn't see my way to do it. I'm so sorry.' The image of a sneering Derek flashed into her mind. She had been a coward, thinking only of her job and the precious reputation of the college and so on and so forth. If she had spoken up in time, could she have prevented what happened to Oliver?

'Believe me,' said St. Just, 'the reputation of the college will suffer much more if there's a lingering mystery about who killed the master, and now who killed Oliver Staunton. You do see that, don't you? The conspiracy theorists are probably already accusing random people on social media or in some podcast or other. Reputations and lives are being destroyed. Which is why, of course, we need to find the real culprit and we need to find that person very soon.

'So anything you can tell me, do. Tell me everything. And let me decide what is important or not.'

'The thing is,' she began, 'the thing is, you see, he was very upset at finding the master, so he wasn't making a great deal of sense, Oliver wasn't.'

'So you did talk about it. At length?'

'Of course we talked about it! Everyone was just agog with it. There was very little else to talk about when it happened and even now – well, I'd say now it's going to be worse.'

'In what way worse?'

'They're all angling for a place, you see. A position. All the dons, all the people with a long attachment to the college, all the ones with ambition – which is all of them. The mastership of Hardwick College would be a feather in the cap of so many. Some of them would be deserving of it on merit or longevity, of course, but some are only deserving because they want it so badly. And they're the ones who are liable to win out.'

'I am familiar with the phenomenon,' said St. Just. 'Do you really think this has something to do with the murder? Someone wanting to gain advantage by killing the master? To take his place?'

'I don't know,' she said softly. 'I only know Oliver had it in his head that Professor Patricia Beadle-Batsford – Professor Pat, as we call her – had her eye on the prize for a long time. And the fact of her being a woman was her running platform, if you follow.'

'I believe I do. She wanted to redress the imbalance of centuries of discrimination. Is she qualified for the position?'

'Who knows?' Zola shrugged. 'Are any of them, really? Most of them are academics and those are not the most practical people, generally speaking. You go to them if you want to count angels dancing on the head of a pin, that sort of thing. What's really needed is a business head to keep the old place running in the black.'

Where, wondered St. Just, is a Thomas Cromwell when you need him?

'Are you saying, though, Ms Blaze, that Oliver had some particular reason for thinking your "Professor Pat" was involved?'

'He told me he thought he saw her that night. Before, you know, the bell tolled and he heard the scream and he went to see what was happening.'

'Do you mean to tell me he had a first-hand sighting of

someone acting suspiciously, maybe someone who shouldn't
have been there at all, and he kept that to himself?'

'He wasn't sure, he told me. Look, between us, Oliver had
a bit of a run-in with the law a long way back. He had issues
as a young man. I think he had a bit of a wild streak. He went
into the army, straightened himself out, had a good career.
Maybe he drank a bit – never on the job, I'm sure of that, but
he lived in fear this old stuff would come back to haunt him.
He wanted nothing to do with the police – ever. And he sure
as heck wasn't going to throw anyone to the wolves unless he
was one hundred per cent certain he had seen that person. And
it was too dark, his eyesight was too bad, not to mention his
hearing, and he just couldn't be sure.'

'He told you all this?'

'The morning after the night it all happened, yes.'

'Exactly what did he see? What did he tell you?'

She spoke slowly, reaching into her memory for the words
Oliver had used. 'It was right after the bell toll at eleven fifteen.
Maybe twenty after. He saw what he thought was a student.'

'Male or female?'

'He couldn't tell, they were covered up. He thought it was
a new student because he or she was wearing their academic
cap and gown. Honestly, no one does that outside of matriculation and graduation. Absolutely no one wanders around in
their gowns. It's considered to be showing off and they'd be
a laughingstock if anyone saw them. But this was someone
– this was Oliver's take on it – someone using the gown as a
disguise, and especially the cap. Not a mortarboard; it's a flat
medieval thing made of some felted material. It was pulled
down low, and the hair had been tucked into it so you couldn't
tell whether they were male or female, and they were wearing
a mask – a black, medical-style mask as people still do since
Covid.'

'And what did this person do?'

'They crossed First Court and went into Second. Oliver
thought nothing of that; that would naturally be where a student
would go. But then they came right back. He saw them come
back into First Court, dodging the cameras, he thought – those
useless cameras – and starting for the Master's Lodge.'

'And then what?'

'And then Oliver heard the phone ring in the Porters' Lodge. Of course, he practically *threw* himself on the phone, thinking it was that eejit grandson of his. Turns out, it wasn't. It was from a spammer, in fact, but Oliver's job is to answer the phone no matter what, and so he ran off to do that.'

'And that's all? He never saw the robed figure going in or out of the Master's Lodge?'

She shook her head. 'You see? You see why he didn't tell you? You see why *I* didn't tell you? It just seemed to have nothing to do with that scream he heard at midnight, and there was really nothing solid to pass along.'

'The time of death is up to the pathologist to determine. It's something the police need to pinpoint as closely as possible before we can get anywhere. This information doesn't move that needle but it gives us another potential witness, wouldn't you say? Or suspect?'

'Yes, I do. And I am sorry – you're right, I know you're right. It was probably one of the foreign students, if that narrows it down for you. They are the ones who are so proud of that regalia that they wear it at all the wrong times. They probably sleep in it.'

Or use it as a bathrobe, thought St. Just. Although that would show more contempt than pride.

'What made Oliver think it was Professor Pat?'

'He said whoever it was walked like they were tied to a pole. If you've ever seen her walk, ramrod straight, you know what he meant. And it was a thin, slight person. But of course, he realized it could have been a student.' She glanced down at her stomach, where the baby fat had come to live. 'They all look thin to me.'

St. Just considered. He would need to have someone speak with whoever oversaw admissions for the newest uptake of students. How many of them would there be? Three hundred? Four hundred? He sighed. It was hopeless, but there was no way around it. The physical description she'd just relayed might narrow it down.

Today's more immediate task would be to narrow the time of death of the porter. They knew it was presumably between the hours of ten p.m. when he came on duty, and six a.m. when Zola arrived, and more likely between ten and midnight if Oliver had indeed locked the gate as he should have done. Unless his murderer was a student.

Ten p.m., of course, was when Evans, the afternoon and evening porter, finished his shift.

That would be another interview. He wondered briefly if he would ever see Portia again until after this case was closed.

'We'll have to get a statement from you, to include your whereabouts during the estimated times of these murders. Just a formality, you understand.'

She nodded.

He was determined this would not be an open-ended case with no resolution, and nothing but speculation to fuel it down the decades.

As if reading his thoughts, Zola was saying, 'There's already a podcast out there about the master's being killed. I wonder how legal that could be. People have a right to their opinions, of course, but isn't there a line that gets crossed when they start conjuring up theories targeting random strangers?'

'Just out of curiosity, whom are they accusing?'

'They aren't naming names yet, but the theories range from a love affair gone wrong, including massive speculation about the master's sexual orientation, all the way up to an international cabal interested in stealing his art collection for a Russian oligarch.'

'He was a known private collector then?'

'To the extent his salary would allow,' she said, 'of course he was. He loved all that old stuff. It was his life.'

'But nothing along the lines of, say, a rare Rembrandt?'

'One of the podcasts picked up on that angle. That article online in the local paper, you know. You must've seen it.'

'Yes,' he said briefly.

He didn't suppose it was a case yet for Interpol, but what if this had everything to do with missing artwork? It had to be followed up, and quickly.

Again, he sighed. The manpower just wasn't there. And now – all eyes had to be on this latest death.

'What about the unrequited love angle, or whatever you mentioned?'

'Personally, I would say that was a dead end,' Zola said. 'Pardon the expression. The man did not have a personal life to speak of. No wife or children, no lover – believe me, I would know, and for sure, Oliver would've known. There are no secrets like that to be kept at Hardwick College. The night shift is where all the, you know, action takes place – if it's going to. Not during daylight hours. I just get the ones who've lost their jumpers or mislaid their keys.'

St. Just thought she had just given him the obvious clue as to why the porter had been murdered. He was perfectly positioned to witness any shady goings-on at night. The afternoon and evening porter, Evans, had less to witness and Zola, the day porter, even less than that. The wonder was that Zola hadn't been given Oliver's shift, as being more likely to stay awake.

Again, she seemed to be tracking his thoughts. She said, 'The master did ask me once if I wanted the night shift, but I had childcare to think of. I need to be with Lucille at night. He was very understanding, but the fact he asked suggests maybe he did pay more attention to practical matters than I had thought. Anyway, Oliver was up to the job. There was no crime going on at the college, not up until the master was killed. It was more young love and larking about and all that.'

'Sky-walking.'

'You know about that, then? Yes. He just let things like that roll off him. Which made him better at the job than I would have been, if I'm honest. I'd have read them the riot act and sent them home to their nannies.'

'And you're quite certain Oliver was, as the saying goes, of sound mind.'

'Absolutely. Test that gun and Oliver's hands for residue. You'll see.'

He nodded. Based solely on her testimony, he now firmly believed this was no suicide.

This was another murder.

SIXTEEN
See No Evil

S t. Just left Zola Blaze in the senior common room being comforted by the cleaning woman, who had easily been persuaded to set aside her mop and pail and share a fresh cuppa. Zola, with her office roped off with crime scene tape, had nowhere to be that day anyway.

The Porters' Lodge would officially be closed until further notice. Students were being instructed to enter the grounds via the car park round the side. He wondered how many of them were uploading podcasts or being interviewed for a vlog (he was trying to learn the jargon; it was embarrassing to interview a young witness and not have a clue what they were on about) even as he made his way through First Court to the Porters' Lodge. He had instructed his team to block off the entire First Court to avoid selfie-taking photographers, but there was nothing to prevent them going up to the roof and photographing the scene from up there. He supposed he should block it off also, but they weren't interfering with the actual crime scene.

He had a sudden thought. Or were they? Hastily, he sent a text to Sergeant Fear.

Bar entry to the roof around the First Court immediately, he wrote. It was a painstaking process because he used one index finger rather than both thumbs to text. In the same way he used the keyboard on his computer. *And text me the home address for the third porter ASAP. He's named Evans. Then meet me there.*

The response was almost immediate. The address proved to be in the southern part of town in a row of terraced houses with neat gardens in front. It wasn't the poshest or priciest part of the city, but it was an area where keeping up appearances was valued. The home of Aled Evans had a door painted blue and a polished doorknocker of a jumping dolphin. Since they were miles from the sea, St. Just wondered if the inhabitants had brought the knocker back from holiday or had inherited it from a seafaring relative.

The man who answered the door was massive, making the near-newborn in his large, muscled arms look even tinier. He wore a T-shirt designed to highlight his bulging biceps; one forearm bore a tattoo of a knotted Celtic design. The baby regarded the policemen with unseeing blue eyes from under a thatch of blond hair that stood out in random tufts. By anyone's standards he was an adorable child, and even more adorably, a quiet one.

'You've come about Oliver, haven't you?' asked Aled Evans. 'Of course you have. Zola texted me. I can't believe this.' The baby tilted back its head and watched its father's face, sensing that something distressing was being discussed. Probably it could feel his father's heartbeat quicken.

'Please come in,' said Aled, stepping back. 'I'm afraid I don't have a great deal to tell you. My shift is from two in the afternoon until ten at night when Oliver picks up the slack. *Picked* up the slack. Should I come into the college? Pitch in to help?'

'For now, there is no Porters' Lodge, so you and Zola can rest easy. The students and visitors will have to fend for themselves. We do have a few questions.'

'Certainly.' He pointed their way into a front room bursting with baby gear.

'How long have you been at Hardwick College?' asked St. Just, pausing to glance at the display of family photos in the hall. The baby took after its mother in size and blondness.

'Ten years now,' said Aled. 'After the army. Take a seat.'

'Now, everything was as usual when you last saw Oliver before he started his shift that evening?' asked St. Just. He and Fear settled into two overstuffed chairs after clearing them of baby debris. When did babies come to need so much equipment?

'Absolutely. If anything, he was a bit more cheery than usual. He'd heard from the grandson at last. Gerry. Praise heaven.' The last words, accompanied by an eye-roll, were heavy with sarcasm. Apparently, the man wasn't any fonder of Gerry than was Zola Blaize.

St. Just supposed it wasn't important, but he asked, 'Did Oliver say when he heard from him, the grandson?'

'No. Does it matter?'

Sergeant Fear spoke for the first time. 'Everything matters, sir,' he said politely.

'Of course. Can I offer you both some coffee?' asked Aled. 'Someone will have to hold Tomos. I find I can manage most things and not drop him, but not the new coffee maker.'

'Give him to me,' said Sergeant Fear, putting down his notebook and holding out his hands. 'I have one about this size at home.'

The baby went through the transfer of ownership without a struggle, perhaps enjoying the change of routine. The two policemen and Tomos settled back and took in their surroundings. It was a typical working man's cottage which had been upgraded, with mixed results. It retained a certain charm and was undeniably pleasant, but much that was authentic had been covered up by plasterboard and bright paint.

The original features consisted of a brick fireplace and heavy wood doors. These had been sanded and painted bright blue, yellow and red. Somehow St. Just associated this colour scheme with the arrival of the baby. It was believed to stimulate their senses to have all these vivid colours round them.

Aled Evans returned with a tray holding three filled coffee mugs. He took the chipped brown one for himself. The other two were souvenirs showing his support for the Cambridge Rugby Club.

'I'll tell you why we're here,' said St. Just. 'I am beginning to realize how much the porters at a college are the very heart and soul of the place. Also the eyes and ears. Little goes on that you don't know about, does it?' This bit of flattery was probably the truth, and it had the desired effect.

Retrieving his child from Fear, Aled said, 'You'd be right there. We are the soul of discretion, of course. But we do see everything.'

'So what did you see and what do you know in connection
with the master's death?'

'I know that he didn't die at the stroke of midnight. There's
a podcast out there about the murder with that name – "The
Master Died at Midnight"; I ask you – but that's not what
happened.'

'You don't say?' said St. Just. 'And how do you come by
that knowledge?'

'Oliver had seen enough of death in the war to know that
when he found him, the master had been dead for some time.
Oliver couldn't give a precise time, and he'd known enough
not to disturb the body or the scene, but he knew when he
found the master at midnight he hadn't just been killed. That
scream he heard could've been male or female, said Oliver,
but it had not come from the master.'

'Would Oliver have been tempted to keep that to himself?'
When he'd spoken to Zola just now it hadn't sounded as if
Oliver had mentioned this, even though he'd shared much of
his personal background with her. Perhaps he'd compartmen-
talized, saving her for issues where a woman was likely to be
understanding, and sharing the more 'manly' details with
Evans.

'He was a funny guy. You had to know him. He meant no
harm, I'm sure.'

'Lying to the police does a great deal of harm,' Fear pointed
out.

'It wasn't lying, exactly.' Aled addressed his remarks to St.
Just, showing he was clearly another rank-and-file type. 'He
knew the police pathologist would get there sooner or later,
and be more accurate, to boot. It wasn't really his place to be
telling you your job, was it?'

St. Just remembered what Zola had told him about Oliver's
run-in with the law, and thought he understood – maddening
as it was, especially with Oliver now gone. The man wouldn't
want to draw attention to himself by being a know-it-all. It
made perfect sense. But St. Just wondered what else he hadn't
said.

Had Oliver wanted to avoid incriminating someone?
Someone who wanted to encourage police to believe the murder

had taken place at midnight – to establish an alibi? Perhaps
the real answer was he had some suspicion or other about
someone, perhaps even his grandson. Someone whose whereabouts for earlier that night were best obscured.

'Did he mention to you he thought a valuable painting
might've gone missing from the master's office?'

'No. Did one?' Gently, Aled jiggled the baby on his lap,
tucking a blanket round him. He looked across at the policemen,
guileless to all appearances. 'Oliver didn't say.'

'I'm asking what you know, sir.'

'Well, that's just it, isn't it? I know what Oliver told me
and he didn't say anything about paintings. To be sure, the
master had lots of them, but we porters weren't allowed in
for, like, a viewing. We weren't invited in at all except in case
of emergencies. There's an annual party in the senior common
room for staff – that sort of do is never held in the master's
rooms. It would be . . . I don't know. It just isn't done.'

'So Oliver said nothing about artwork to you.' St. Just left
a long pause. Often an interviewee would rush in to fill the
gap, sometimes with gibberish, sometimes with better
information.

'He was nearly knocked for six by the whole thing. I
wouldn't have expected much more than what I got, which
was a frantic relay of information.'

'We would like you to walk us through your shift on the
afternoon of the day the master later died. And if you could
do the same for the day Oliver was killed.'

'You say that as if they aren't related. Is there any chance
of that?'

'I'd say that's highly unlikely.'

'A copycat killing, maybe? They are a highly imaginative
and suggestible group at Hardwick,' said the porter. 'As are
all the people who come to Cambridge, for that matter. I don't
see it as out of the realm of the possible.'

'Neither do I, when you put it that way,' said St. Just. 'But
let's stick with what is evident, why don't we? There's a
connection between the two murders beyond – let's call it –
the coincidental timing. And that's what we're looking for,
that connection. One thing led to another. I think it is beyond

chance that events happened otherwise. That allows for the roving maniac to enter the narrative, and really, how many true maniacs have you seen in Cambridge?'

'You'd be surprised.' The porter sat back, resettling the baby, who had fallen asleep at the comforting rumble of his father's chest. 'All right, we'll start with the master's death. But I can't tell you what happened between ten and midnight, since I wasn't there.'

'Actually, sir, we have reason to believe he was murdered around half past eleven. But you had left the premises at ten, is that correct?'

'More or less. Of course, I can't swear to the minute. There's usually a bit of banter between me and Oliver, some back and forth, chewing the fat. You know the kind of thing; he filled me in on what had happened that night, just as I would fill Zola the day porter in on what had happened during my shift. My shift that day was slow. A slow afternoon followed by a slow evening.'

'Oliver told us that you saw the master go out for the evening. Is that true?'

'Yes. I'd nearly forgotten about that. He went to dine at another college.'

'That would be King's, correct?'

'I don't really know.'

'Did he say where he was going?'

Aled shook his head, looking down at Tomos. 'He wasn't required to sign in and out like a visitor. And it wasn't my business to know the master's business.'

'No matter, sir, we have verified reports that he was at the dinner.' St. Just did not add that after interviewing Zola he'd received an email telling him the master had been seen at a local pub around six thirty having a drink alone before the college dinner. A couple of witnesses recognized him but apart from drinking alone – a single glass of wine – his actions were unremarkable.

'Also,' St. Just added, 'we know what time he was thought to have left the dinner.' The local policeman – Abelard, the one who so got up Fear's nose – had been deputized to speak to the caterer over at King's, who reported that the master had left straight after the dinner at nine o'clock. He had not joined the other high table diners in the SCR afterwards for claret and coffee, as would be usual.

It wasn't required that he be there, the caterer had explained. Just expected.

The master wouldn't need a full hour to return to his nearby college. What might he have been doing?

'So,' St. Just continued, 'we know he must've arrived back at Hardwick College around ten, perhaps even earlier? At nine forty-five?' St. Just was fishing to see if Aled's story changed.

'Again, he's not required to sign in or report his doings to me. But you say he was killed later, and that makes sense to me.'

'Why do you say that?'

'Because there's still a bit of commotion in the Second and Third Courts late at night. Some of the newer students, you know. I would expect a clever murderer to have waited until dark. I mean, *really* dark, when everything was still and the students were all snuggled in their beds. Wouldn't you?'

'It's a thought,' St. Just said noncommittally.

'Of course, there's the occasional sky-walker, but not on my shift.'

'I'd like to have the names of the students going in for that.'

'And I'd like to tell you, but if it happens, it happens quite late at night. Sorry, I can't help you. And I don't know what Oliver may have known, come to that. He never spoke of it.'

'I see. And there's no more you can tell us about the master's return to the college that night?'

The porter shook his head before answering. 'There's a certain ritual in handing over the keys to Oliver and reporting on what happened, even when the report is "Nothing Happened". Tradition, you know.'

'*Rien*, as King Louis might say, as if the guillotine hadn't been invented. You mean literally – you hand over the keys?'

'Yes, of course. You see, a lot of the keys to the older doors are one-of-a-kind, centuries old. You can't just have copies made. Well, you could, I suppose, but no one has ever bothered. It's hardly a ceremony with a marching band like the Changing of the Guard at Buckingham Palace, but there's this whole tradition of the porters at Hardwick College handing the keys back and forth.'

St. Just found this interesting but didn't see how it played into the events of the night, except Oliver had told police he'd started to let himself into the Master's Lodge using a key, then discovered the door was unlocked and was in fact standing open by a fraction of an inch.

What Aled Evans was telling them was that no one else was likely to have such a key. It would require a true locksmith, not just a locksmith but an antiquarian expert, to reproduce anything that might work.

Something connected in his mind at the thought – the gun suppressor that may have been used on the gun that killed Oliver.

'So you couldn't swear to seeing the master return? I'm quite certain Oliver thought you had.' This was not actually true, but he was interested to see Aled's reaction.

'I'm not lying.' The baby stirred in his father's arms, once again picking up signals that something was amiss. It was like having a tiny lie detector tucked against one's chest. St. Just chose to let it go.

'You allowed Mr Ambrose Nussknacker in, did you not? As a visitor to see the master in the evening.'

'Yes, that'll be in the logbook. It was five or thereabouts.'

'You saw Nussknacker leave?'

'I signed him out.'

'That's not what I asked.'

'Yes, I saw him leave. I signed him out.'

'Very well. Then you left for home after the shift change and later heard the news about the master's death. Who did you hear it from?'

'From Oliver. I think he must've called me right after he called your lot, or maybe the other way round. He was really not himself.'

'Now we come to the night Oliver was killed.'

Aled Evans shook his head and said, 'Do you know, I've been racking my brains, wondering what I might have missed.'

'Again, nothing out of the ordinary?'

'No. When I come on duty, at two in the afternoon, it is always slow. It picks up in the evening. That's when they're all jamming into the outer porter's lodge to check their pigeon-holes for invitations, news, supervision cancellations, and the usual. Since they mostly use text or email, our job is lightened in that regard. There is still the odd student who likes to carry on as if they're starring in *Brideshead Revisited*, passing along notes on fancy paper and leaving calling cards and so on.'

'Wrong university,' Sergeant Fear commented.

The porter looked at him. 'Yes, I know, Sergeant. Anyway, Hardwick is not the sort of place where everyone's gone mental trying to outdo everyone else. Not all the students are nobs, you know. They're from all over, from everywhere, all walks of life. As it should be.'

'I wasn't trying to be clever, sir,' said Fear.

'Sorry,' said Aled. 'I think this business has upset me more than I like to admit. But you see, it reflects badly on the college, and on those of us whose job it is to protect the college. It's an utter failure in that regard.'

'So, let's say the rush for you ends about seven in the evening?' St. Just asked, moving them past the moment.

'That would be fair to say. Maybe eight o'clock.'

'And then you have two hours to watch the telly, check the mobile phone for messages?'

'That about sums it up.'

'And then Oliver turns up, you do the handing-over-the-keys ritual, you go home, and he does his general routine?'

'Yes.'

'And what is that routine, do you know?'

Aled sighed. 'If you want my best guess, he goes into the little sitting area behind the reception desk, turns on the telly, and nods off. I may as well tell you straight, he wasn't as alert as he used to be, and absolutely no one wanted to call him on it because it didn't matter. That college is safe as houses. Or it was, until now.'

'So, someone could sneak into the sitting area and attack him while he was asleep?'

'Unless he locked himself inside, yes. He would've closed

the door for privacy, but that doesn't mean he locked it. I doubt he would have.'

That matched what the police found at the scene, thought St. Just. There was no sign of forced entry.

'So,' said Aled, 'you think he was just watching whatever was on the telly that time of night and someone approached him from behind? And shot him?'

'That's about the size of our thinking.'

'Are you definitely ruling out suicide then? Zola was unyielding on that.'

St. Just said with more confidence than he felt, 'Yes, sir, we are.'

As they were leaving the home of Aled Evans, St. Just said to Fear, 'He wasn't telling the whole story, was he?'

'I didn't think so, sir. These porters stick together, don't they? It's clear Oliver was well liked by his comrades. No one wants to dump him in it, whether it be suicide or murder.'

'There's a bit of contradiction in what Oliver told us about the night he found the master dead. Do you have it in your notes?'

'Yes.' Fear waited until they were both back sitting in the car. He found the relevant page and read back the words to St. Just.

'You asked Oliver Staunton: "Did Evans say he'd seen the master come in at ten?"'

'And Oliver replied: "He was already in the back room here, getting ready to leave, shouting out something to me about the schedule for next week, so he didn't see him, no."'

Fear added, 'Oliver also said: "Evans said the master went out for dinner but he wasn't sure where or what time."'

'That dinner information tallies with what Aled Evans told us. But . . .'

'But the business about the master's return . . . It's the same but not exactly,' said Sergeant Fear. 'Either Aled saw him, or he didn't, and he rather avoided the question. From what we're learning, Oliver might had been trying to protect Aled from scrutiny.'

'It might be nothing,' said St. Just. 'It was an ordinary night for the man just doing his job, and perhaps he's really not sure. We know the master didn't come straight back to the college after dinner unless he slipped unseen past Aled, which would mean Oliver was lying about seeing the master return at ten. Or they both were lying. What we do know is the master left the dinner early. Surely that was a bit rude, for one of these formal dos?'

'Maybe he had an early appointment in the morning. Or he was not feeling well. Or he was just being eccentric. I'm sure they're used to that.'

'Or maybe he had a late meeting that night,' said St. Just. 'While Oliver was asleep, all sorts of hell may have broken loose. If he woke up, he might have thought he heard something on the telly and thought nothing of it.'

'It's possible . . .'

'The more we learn, the more I think we're overlooking something,' continued St. Just. 'The painting of the young woman that was there is gone – Constable Broadhurst has confirmed nothing like that is on her list – and, unless that's a red herring, it's why the master was killed. We don't even know if it was a valuable painting, but we assume it was, or at least that someone *thought* it was.

'It wasn't a large painting so it would be easy enough to smuggle out, especially if someone was wearing one of those billowing scholars' robes.'

'Or one of those fancy gowns like the professors wear,' said Fear.

'Of course. We can't forget that the master had been at a formal dinner. We need to find out what the formal regalia is for someone of his level at Hardwick College. A search of the website for Ryder and Amies ought to do it.'

'In case he was seen wearing it. Maybe CCTV can still be our friend.'

'We've been thinking someone sneaked in, but what if they sneaked in as themselves but *left* as the master? Wearing his gown and concealing what they'd stolen.' He paused. 'The more I think about it, the more likely it seems. The team found an academic gown in his rooms and I had them make sure it went to forensics, but maybe it wasn't Sir Flyte's. Maybe someone did a swap. Get someone to check on that would you, Fear? The killer may have left something for forensics to find. Have them look again around the master's rooms. We may be missing something . . .'

'What?' said Fear.

'I'm not sure. But we should have been checking the nearby rubbish bins. And any cameras in their vicinity.'

SEVENTEEN
You Don't Say

As Fear drove, St. Just took out his mobile to dial Portia. The call went straight to voicemail, so he left a message asking her to arrange a meeting with her colleague, Annalise Bellagamba, the expert in art theft and forgery.

The rain promised by forecasters had begun, a moderate sprinkling the intermittent wipers could easily manage, rather than the promised flooding rain. But the weather had been so changeable that the Cambridge area had recently been under several yellow warnings.

'I wonder exactly how this missing painting came into the hands of the master of Hardwick College,' he said to Sergeant Fear. 'And how that plays into his murder, if it does. We need to clear up this art angle, and I'm not sure the real and unbiased expert we need to talk to is Ambrose Nussknacker.'

'I would agree,' said Fear. 'He's too bound up in the situation, isn't he? It's like asking a fox about the welfare of the chickens.'

'I do enjoy your homespun expressions, Sergeant. One would almost think you grew up on a farm.'

Not certain if he was being teased, Fear said, 'City born and bred. But our neighbour keeps chickens.'

'That must be a nuisance for you. Meanwhile, we need to follow up on some of these alibis. It seems to me there was a regular parade of people to and from the Master's Lodge that night, and I don't think that was a regular occurrence. Oliver indicated the master mostly stayed home quietly at night.'

'You're right, sir,' said Sergeant Fear. 'I've been having the same thought about the foot traffic. What's needed here is a spreadsheet to track what happened and what we think happened and when.'

St. Just replied, 'The spreadsheet in my head starts out like this: the master returns at ten, or thereabouts. If he left the dinner at King's around nine that night, and we have been told by numerous sources that's when the dinner ended, then there is too much time unaccounted for. It's perhaps a five-minute walk back to Hardwick College from King's. So, where was he?'

'The security cameras haven't picked up anything unusual for that time of night,' said Fear. 'It's possible he went along the Backs by the river instead of along King's Parade as we've been assuming. There are far fewer cameras along the Backs – and it's dark, anyway. It is a difficult area to patrol, as you know.'

'Let's say he headed east out of town. Where would that land him?'

'It would land him within five to ten minutes in the neighbourhood of Professor Patricia Beadle-Batsford,' answered Fear promptly.

'So, nine twenty at most, let's say. He arrives at the professor's house. The party is in full swing. We were told two stories about the washing-up from Patricia and her daughter, Peyton. That kind of routine daily activity might be easy to mix up in remembrance, but honestly, for anyone close to the master, or those who had made his acquaintance, it is one that should stand out clearly in their minds – the man was murdered practically on their doorstep, after all. It seems a significant contradiction that for Peyton and her mother, the details don't seem to have lodged in their memories. I'd like to get to the bottom of why.'

'Right you are, guv.'

'Anyway, here is the master, either in full dining regalia or, more likely, holding his gown and hood over his arm, making his way along a badly lit part of the river up to the area where Dr Pat resides. What does he do when he gets there? I suppose we could put out a call for witnesses who may have seen him along the river, but that won't answer the question of what he thought he was doing. I think that's a thread we need to follow up. If he wanted to talk to Dr Pat, he could've done so at any time during normal daylight hours. It has all the elements of a spy mission, doesn't it?'

'A spy mission?' said Sergeant Fear, making a slightly misjudged turn to avoid the traffic around the city centre.

'Yes, a spy mission. He knew there was something going on, and he didn't trust anyone to tell him what it was, so he went to see for himself. Something like that. Perhaps Ambrose said something to him about it earlier. He may have found it rather embarrassing or felt slightly ridiculous, but he had to find out.'

'Do you think Sir Flyte might have been trying to catch someone in the act of something? Something related to the painting?'

'We only have two options. It's either about the painting, or it's about something else that we haven't uncovered yet.'

'Now, there's a wide field. Anyway, shall I get a team to canvas the area around the river, especially near the professor's house? To find out if anyone saw the master that night?'

'All right, yes, and run the recordings from the security cameras. While you do that, I'll keep trying to arrange the meeting with Portia's art expert at the Institute of Criminology. We need to know more about this missing painting. Nearly everything seems to circle round it.'

'Will do.'

'What time is it getting to be?' He looked at his watch to answer his own question. 'It's getting on for noon. Can you swing by Peyton's restaurant? What was the name?'

'Virtue.' Once again, Sergeant Fear executed a marginally legal U-turn, taking them back half the way they had come.

'Should we mark this as official?' he asked, pulling into a spot near the restaurant and reaching for the 'police business' placard.

'No, we'll do this by the book, more or less. Wait here for me and send parking away with a flea in their ear if they bother you. But before I go, read back to me from your notes what Peyton said regarding her movements the night the master was killed – her movements after the dinner party ended. During the winding down of the party, they all alibi each other, with the men standing about in the garden having a cigar.'

For the second time that day, Fear flipped back through the pages of his notebook.

'Here it is. "I did the washing-up" – this was after the dinner party – "and went to bed".'

St. Just nodded. 'Right,' he said. 'And the mother told us they did the washing-up together.' Fear began flipping through his notes again, and St. Just said, 'No need for that. I am certain that is what the professor told us. Rufus told us the party ended about quarter to eleven.'

He got out of the car, dug in his pockets, and dutifully inserted a half-hour's worth of coins into the machine. These coin-operated machines were vanishing from Cambridge, replaced by apps. St. Just hated apps.

He walked into the premises of Virtue, a fashionable restaurant he had planned for ages to take Portia to. He asked the first server he saw if he could speak to Peyton and was shown to a seat near the kitchen. He ordered a coffee. The restaurant was completely empty of customers.

She emerged from the back about ten minutes later, wiping her hands on a dish towel.

'Well, this is a surprise, Inspector. What's up?'

'Perhaps you haven't heard, so I'm sorry to have to tell you. The night porter over at Hardwick College has died.'

'Mr Staunton? You don't mean murdered?'

'We're not one hundred per cent certain, but yes. We think so. Interesting that you made the same connection the police did. That there were too many people at that college dying in a row for it to be a coincidence.'

She pulled out a chair, scraping its legs against the floor, and sat down hard across from him. 'How did he die?'

'That's to be determined,' he said. 'Now, I want you to tell me again what you were doing the night the master was murdered.'

She caught her breath momentarily. Surely she had anticipated this, but she replied smoothly, 'As I told you, I did the washing-up after the dinner party and went to bed.' That was her story, word for word, and she was sticking to it.

'Your mother told us you did the washing-up together.'

'You know, I don't really remember,' she said quickly – too quickly. 'Perhaps. Yes, I think so.'

'Have you ever been inside the Master's Lodge?'

'What? No. I wasn't a student at the college for very long, and besides, the students don't get invited over for tea with the master – except under extraordinary circumstances, I guess. Nobles and such.'

'You and your mother wouldn't be trying to create an alibi for each other, would you?'

She let out a brief laugh, relieved at the change of topic. 'You really don't know the ins and outs of our relationship, do you? But as it happens, I wouldn't do that for anybody. I'm a real law-and-order type. Ask anyone. Now if there's nothing else? The lunch crowd is starting to arrive and there's a large group—'

'Just bring me the bill. The coffee is delicious, by the way.'

She waved that away. 'It's on the house.'

'No, I insist. Otherwise, it's a bribe. As a law-and-order type, you must appreciate that.'

She went to the waiter's station and returned with a payment gadget, as St. Just thought of it. The proper name eluded him. It was one of those devices into which you inserted your credit card and signed using your finger.

He had trouble with it, inserting his card this way and that with no response. Losing patience, she took it from his hands and inserted the card properly so he could sign.

Once back at the car, he showed his credit card to Sergeant Fear, holding it gingerly at the edges.

'We've got her fingerprints now. If she was in the Master's Lodge and she's lying about it, we'll know.'

Catching Fear's look, for Fear was indeed a law-and-order type, he said, 'We'll do a visual against the prints they found when they dusted the master's office. If it looks like a match to the naked eye, we'll ask her voluntarily for her prints for elimination purposes. No one would refuse such an innocent and potentially helpful request. And if they do . . .'

'We've got her,' said Fear. 'But do you really think . . .?'

'Do I really think she's a killer? Who can say, about anyone, under the "right" circumstances? But if she's lying, we really need to know why.'

EIGHTEEN
To Catch a Thief

The reigning expert on art theft and forgery breezed into the room where Sergeant Fear and DCI St. Just had been asked to wait. She arrived as a blur of colour. Her dress – a kaleidoscopic pattern – was topped with a bright red jacket, a hue that enhanced her dark eyes and warm complexion. They all introduced themselves. She had brought them coffee from the break room.

'Do not expect much,' she warned them. 'We had to petition for the room, and we are only incrementally increasing our demands for ventilation, decent coffee, real milk and a refrigerator to keep it in. And a lock on the door to keep out students.'

'Portia had mentioned the innovation to me,' said St. Just. 'Apparently the meetings over it were rather intense. I shouldn't be surprised if a heavily redacted account were to appear in one of her future crime novels, with names changed to protect the innocent.'

'You have no idea,' said Professor Annalise Bellagamba. 'You have a prize there in Portia,' she added.

St. Just beamed. 'Don't I know it?'

'How can I help you today? I know it's to do with the death of Flyte Rascallian over there at Hardwick College.'

'Unfortunately, our mandate has expanded to include the night porter. Oliver Staunton.'

'Oh good gracious. You mean . . . he's dead? What in the world? Poor man. Poor both of them. I didn't know the porter, except in passing on my way to High Table of an evening – Sir Flyte was good enough to invite me on several occasions – but let me tell you, Flyte was a friend, and I feel his loss perhaps even more than his other colleagues and students do. A brain like his doesn't come along every century. He really was one of the best in his field.'

'Ah,' said St. Just. 'His intelligence is not in question. But how would you rate him as a human being?'

'Oh, these artificial constructs!' she said. 'But with Flyte, yes, it was all business all the time. I don't think I can quite separate out the strands of his personality for you. He lived for art, particularly the Old Masters, particularly Rembrandt. If he was talking about his pet subject, he was warm and animated. I had this theory, you see . . .'

'Oh, yes?'

'That part of what he admired about Rembrandt is the way he lived his life in a don't-give-a-damn way. And Sir Flyte, given his position, was never allowed to do so.'

'And outside of – shall we call it his obsession?'

'Outside of his love of art, Flyte could be a bit distant. He was, as I say, a friend, but even with me it was always "Sir Flyte" to his face, never simply "Flyte". He had trouble connecting with people who didn't share his passion. I suppose he thought they were dolts – who wouldn't love art? Don't get me wrong. He was always perfectly polite and correct – *frightfully* British, you know.' She exaggerated the word, slipping into an upper-class accent. 'I am Italian, as no doubt you can hear, so perhaps I felt this more than most, but there was a sort of . . . a solitary loneliness to him. Yes, that's the best way to say it. Perhaps he wasn't like that as a young man. Most of us have at least three or four chapters in our lives where our personality expands or shrinks into itself.'

'You say you were a close friend, though,' said St. Just.

'I didn't say "close", but I would call it that, yes. I don't mean to say he confided everything to me, but he did drop hints that I don't think other people were privy to.'

'Did he discuss that he'd inherited some paintings when his aunt passed?'

'He didn't, but I don't suppose he had time. He did tell me he was going to the funeral – he had to cancel coffee with me. Then he was killed shortly afterwards.'

'So you don't know anything about the paintings that came to him?'

'Beyond that rather rubbishy article online? No.'

'Why do you say rubbishy?'

'I mean the reporter was trying to make drama out of nothing, I suppose. Suggestions of a rare Rembrandt. An uncatalogued treasure.'

'You don't think it could be true?'

'I think it would be extremely rare. Not *impossible*, but rare. And the master would have known what he had, or at least have suspected, and would have taken steps to secure it. Why – was it stolen?'

'So it would appear.'

'*Mio Dio.*'

'Do you think securing the painting would have included lying about it to nosy parkers?'

She smiled. 'Yes. Especially once that reporter got wind of it and told the world. The master didn't want his lodge broken into, did he?'

'*Could* it have been a Rembrandt, do you think?'

She shrugged. 'Crazier things have happened. The art world can be very *sub rosa*. Not long ago some items from the British Museum – small items that had not been properly registered – showed up on eBay. The theft would almost certainly have gone undiscovered had items that *were* catalogued not started showing up. They were easy to verify against the inventory. Even then . . .'

'Even then, what?'

'Well, they didn't rush to announce it. It is terrible publicity for a museum or gallery to broadcast that they've been victimized. More goes on in the art world that we don't know about than what we do.'

'You indicated the master had confided in you,' said St. Just. 'We need to know if anything in his background plays into what happened to him.'

'He made vague references to his past, in passing, over the years I'd known him. For example, we might be admiring a painting in a museum together, speculating about its authenticity or its provenance, and he would say something like – looking at a painting by Rembrandt especially – he would say, *clearly* moved, "She looks so much like someone I used to know." And the way he said it . . . Well, call me a romantic, but there was some feeling there. Not just the beauty of the painting itself, something more personal. In fact, one time when he made a reference like that, I said, "You mean someone from your youth?" And he said, "I don't think I ever really had a youth. But if you mean someone from the past, yes."'

'How intriguing. He said nothing more specific?'

'He said, and I'm struggling to remember, it was just a conversation in passing, you know, but he said something like, "The eyes. Deep and far apart like that. And the colouring. That's all." And then he changed the subject.'

St. Just and Fear exchanged glances.

'Well, that's intriguing,' said St. Just. 'Do you happen to remember what painting?'

'I remember very well. It was Rembrandt's famous *Bathsheba at Her Bath*.'

'What can you tell us about it?'

'I can do better than that,' Annalise Bellagamba said. 'I can show you.'

She left the room, returning shortly with a large art book, open to the relevant page, showing a reproduction image of a Rembrandt painting.

'It is an image of his mistress – or I should say, one of them. Rembrandt had quite a chequered past. Loads of trouble with women. After his wife died, he had to hire someone to take care of his child. One thing led to another, and one lawsuit with his wife's family led to another lawsuit. Then another nurse came along, young and pretty . . . it's quite the story. He basically became a bankrupt, but the two mistresses we know of served as his models for many paintings. The paintings aren't always labelled, and there's some dispute about it, but there's little question in my mind this one is Hendrickje Stoffels.'

She pointed at the image with a red-lacquered nail. 'There's a quality of, how would you say, impishness. Mischief. No wonder the old man liked her.'

'Beautiful,' said Sergeant Fear.

'You can barely see her eyes, though,' said St. Just. 'In profile. The mind is distracted by other things.'

'It must have been a wonderful scandal,' said Annalise Bellagamba.

'I would say that,' said St. Just. 'I would also say this doesn't look like anyone I'd expect to find in the master's past. Would you?'

She shrugged. 'You'd be surprised,' she said. 'We didn't really know him. And now we never will.'

Ten minutes later, as Fear and St. Just were leaving the building (another modern horror in St. Just's eyes), Fear said, 'Crikey. I wasn't expecting that.'

'It's a different body type,' said St. Just. 'But the face, the eyes, the colouring – most of all, the attitude. I can see the resemblance, can't you?'

'Yes, indeed. It's Professor Patricia Beadle-Batsford in the altogether – two stone heavier, but it's a strong enough resemblance, minus the impishness. But, perhaps because it's the depiction of a young woman, it looks even more like Peyton, wouldn't you agree?'

'Yes,' said St. Just. 'I think we need to mull all this over carefully. That painting hangs in the Louvre, by the way.'

'Should we read something into Professor Bellagamba's having been with the master in Paris?'

'I don't know. It could have been an innocent outing. But she's dropped lots of hints that there was more to the man that she's not giving away. Let's go somewhere where we can think about where we go next with what we know – rather, what we *think* we know.'

Over coffee at Michaelhouse Café (they hadn't been able to finish the coffee from the break room and had discreetly poured it into a bin at the foot of the steps leading to the Institute of Criminology), St. Just said, 'Constable Broadhurst has just emailed copies of the contents of that briefcase found in the master's rooms. While I try to scroll through all this on my phone, could you put in a call to the station and see what the autopsy report shows on Oliver Staunton? There should be some results from Pomeroy by now that will confirm whether he was a suicide.'

A few minutes later, he overheard Fear leaving a message. 'I'll try Pomeroy again later,' he said.

'Let's ask ourselves why we ignored the fact that the master had a past. We rather assumed he had none. But of course he did, a man his age. Did some entanglement come back to haunt him? Is it possible he had some connection with the Beadle-Batsfords? Pat, in particular? Those were the questions we needed to ask.'

'It's a stretch. Of course, we now have the girl's prints and DNA from her prints, but we can't use them. Not without more evidence than a likeness to an old painting.'

'Right. We'll have to get more evidence, a confession, something to go on. We need to talk to that American chap again. Rufus Penn.'

'But, why?' asked Fear. 'Do you really think he had something to do with this? And if so, what does it have to do with Professor Pat?'

'With her directly, perhaps not much. But her daughter was very much involved with Rufus Penn, and she gave me the impression there's not much she wouldn't do for him.'

'I don't follow your reasoning, sir,' said Fear.

St. Just replied, 'I think you will if we follow up on one comment that he made. About his grandfather and the war. World War Two. Who do we have on the team who's good at trolling through archives and microfilm?'

'Well, there's a few of them. Apart from Broadhurst there's Henderson – our unofficial gun expert. He's big on the war and his grandfather's involvement, has all sorts of trophies and things from the time. Probably a gun or two, but best not ask.'

'He's the man for this. Get him in on it. We need to make the connection between Rufus Penn and the master. Because from some things Rufus said, or avoided saying, I think there was one. We just don't know what it was yet.'

'Texting him now.'

'This case has roots in the past,' St. Just continued. 'Well, of course it does, we're in Cambridge. Everything has roots in the past. But this is something slightly different. And it may have something to do with Rufus's grandfather, or at least, with the war.'

'If I'm honest,' said Fear, 'I don't know what you mean. You simply talked about the dinner with him. And then the cigar business after the dinner. Such a throwback to olden times, wasn't it? But . . . what am I missing?'

'You'll see.' Sergeant Fear found this sort of comment particularly maddening, but when St. Just was working a case, there was no talking to him. The gears would start to turn, like one of those games at a beach arcade.

If you fed it enough coins, out would drop the solution.

NINETEEN
Ancient History

'You told us, sir, that you had come to Cambridge University because your family tradition dictated it.' The policemen had made themselves at home, removing piles of clothing from the two chairs in Rufus Penn's chaotic room. The young man sat across from them on his unmade bed, as before, and did not offer to help or apologize for the mess. He did not look pleased to see them.

'I wouldn't say dictated it. It's a tradition and I have no qualms about following it. I told you before all the reasons this is a great place for someone of my age with my interests.'

'Yes, we'd love to hear more about your interests.'

Perhaps picking up on the tone, Rufus, who normally kept an open, guileless expression, began to shut down. He drew his eyebrows together in a frown. 'Do you know, it might be best if you told me what you were talking about?'

'I had my team do a little climbing up your family tree.'

'Yes, all right. My family is famous so it can't have been hard to do.'

'It seems you have a grandfather who was in the Second World War.'

'Yes, and so?' *Where were they going with this?* From his expression, Rufus couldn't imagine. 'Didn't I tell you that?'

St. Just was beginning to think Rufus's subject should be the theatre rather than art history. The nearby ADC Theatre was missing out on a star performer.

'Can you tell us a bit more about your grandfather?'

He shrugged. 'He was here in Cambridge, during the war. Then after, he volunteered to be part of the mopping up. He would tell us all about it at great length at the drop of a hat. Thanksgivings were a nightmare.' He gave a slight laugh.

Grandfathers! Everyone knew about grandfathers and their war stories.

'Would that more people felt the call to serve,' murmured Sergeant Fear.

Rufus slid his gaze over to meet Fear's eyes and amended his tone. 'He was proud of his service, and, in fact, he performed a very important job for his country and for Europe. What I mean to say is it's no wonder he would never stop talking about it. He had earned the right.'

'What exactly was his contribution to the war effort?' Fear asked.

'You're the one who's been up in my family tree,' replied Rufus.

'Yes, sir, and now we'd really like to hear about it from you,' said St. Just. 'It must've been a rather exciting story.'

'Actually, it was. He became one of the Monuments Men. And I guess you know what that means. In 1943 – hard to believe, almost one hundred years ago now – he volunteered as a young man to help retrieve some of the artworks looted by the Nazis. His background was in rare art. He had specialized knowledge, he also had German-language skills, and he was a natural fit. So they sent him over—'

'Over where, exactly?'

'Well, he ended up going all over Europe. He was with this Allied group from this programme that sent people in small teams to rescue pieces of art and things before the Nazis could destroy or sell them.'

'Monuments, Fine Arts and Archives,' put in Fear.

'Right. There were maybe four hundred of these guys, and my grandfather was one of them. He was very junior, of course. There were museum curators, art historians, architects – all that sort of specialist.'

Warming to his theme, he said, 'At this point, the Nazis had long since scattered, looking to save their own skins. They knew that, for them, the war really was over. But on Hitler's orders, they had been stealing all these irreplaceable artworks and stashing them in places where they couldn't be found or accidentally blown up, even by the Allies. All so that Hitler – the failed artist – could have them for his collection, you understand. It was the worst sort of stolen property, coerced out of people, mostly Jewish people. Not just paintings but tapestries, ornaments, furniture – what have you.'

'Stolen outright.'

'Right. With the owners often sent to the concentration camps. The Monuments Men made it their business to track down these treasures. It wasn't easy, there was no treasure map, but they pieced it together somehow.'

'Men *and* women,' St. Just reminded him.

'Yes, of course, they had women experts as well.' Rufus stopped talking, as if wondering again where this was going. But there was a hunted cast to his wideset eyes that suggested he knew exactly where it was going.

St. Just, for his part, was stalking his prey carefully, slowly, so as not to spook him.

With elaborate politeness, he said, 'If you wouldn't mind terribly, sir, you could be a great help to us in our investigation. As you know, the master was killed soon after acquiring some artwork. We think there is a connection to his death, wouldn't you say? And with your expertise, you might be able to help, much as your grandfather so heroically did.

'What do you know about it – the artwork, I mean?' St. Just went on. 'Or the murder, for that matter. Is there something you may have forgotten to mention?'

Rufus seemed to consider whether he needed to answer at all, but finally he said, 'As to the paintings, I don't know anything about them, except what I read in the papers. There was some thought one was a Rembrandt. Balderdash, as you Brits say.'

'I don't think we actually say it that often. But why do you call it balderdash?'

'Because I think that was just to sell papers, don't you? I mean, that kind of find does happen, but it's rare. People will read the story and scurry up to their attics to see if Uncle Harry left them some Picasso sketch that will fund their retirement. Unless you count broken glass and rocking chairs, there's never anything up there.'

St. Just imagined it would be a different story in the attic of Rufus Penn's house. He had, by this point, seen a photograph on the Internet of the Penn home – correction, one of the Penn's homes – in Rhinebeck, New York. There was also one in the Hamptons, plus a Florida palace that would have pleased Nero with its opulence, and another house in the Bahamas over-looking a turquoise body of water.

'I wish I could help you,' Rufus said, 'but . . .'

The funny thing was, Rufus didn't look at all like he wished he could help them. He kept glancing at his watch.

'If it eases your mind, I've cleared things with your super-visor for today. It's all right if you miss the supervision. He understands it's police business and it's crucial.'

Sergeant Fear, who had been with St. Just all day and knew nothing about this so-called clearance, carefully shielded his gaze. If it got Rufus talking, fine. Otherwise, they could be here forever. A little stick never hurt anyone.

He had learned the art of lying in a good cause from being around St. Just, and realized that was a valuable lesson in and of itself.

'So, all this asking after my grandfather and the war . . . You're implying what exactly?' asked Rufus.

'I'm implying nothing, sir.'

'Yes, you are. My grandfather, I will have you know, was awarded the Congressional Medal of Honor for his work. More than that, I can vouch for his integrity.' He laughed briefly. 'Well, of course I would say that, I'm the grandson, but he was of the generation where his word was his bond, and all of that. I admire him. He was a lot to live up to, and I probably . . . Well, I guess I failed him in that regard. But if you're saying there's something crooked going on, well, you are barking up the wrong family tree, Detective.'

'Inspector,' said St. Just. 'Oh no, sir, I'm not implying that at all. I would just enjoy hearing some of the stories your grandfather must've told you.'

'Very well.' He sighed. 'From an early age he had this interest in art, history, and languages. Like me. So when he realized Roosevelt was initiating this programme – I think it was Roosevelt – he signed up. He had the wherewithal to get by on a small stipend – I mean, he didn't need a salary from Uncle Sam, and most of these volunteers were not in it for the wealth or the glory, anyway. They were outraged by what they saw as the possible eradication of heritage, and they wanted to do what they could to right the wrong. It was dangerous work, as dangerous as going into battle. Not all of them made it out.'

'As you say, a different generation. Good for them.'

'I remember my grandfather saying they needed a car at some point – they were walking and biking everywhere – so he bought them one. He was smart enough to know he needed to make himself useful. Most of these guys were older, you see. Established.'

'And he was younger than you are now.'

'Yes. Anyway, my grandfather was over there several years. He was there when they found this huge cache of treasures in a mine. There's a movie made out of all of this, you know. It's a bit Hollywood-y but they get the broad strokes right.'

'Do you know, I saw it recently. It was streaming on the telly.' He turned to Fear. 'Isn't that how you say it? Streaming?'

Sergeant Fear confirmed it was, suspecting St. Just knew that perfectly well.

'Quite the story. But as I understand it, they couldn't retrieve everything, and some of what was stolen is still out there to be found.'

'Sure,' said Rufus. 'Thousands of works were never recovered. With property worth millions, and human nature being what it is, I guess the temptation was great. Everything was in chaos after the war; people just running to save themselves. People simply wanting souvenirs, for that matter.'

'A Rembrandt would be a whale of a souvenir, wouldn't it?' said St. Just.

'The problem being,' said Rufus, a slight hesitancy in his voice, 'once you've stolen something like that, you need to be well connected with art thieves and forgers to cash it in. You can't just rock up to the National Gallery and ask them if they'd like to have it, or leave it on their doorstep like an abandoned baby, which would not get you the money you want, anyway. There's no finder's fee for something like that, not as with the detectorists, for example, when they find a

Roman hoard. Anyway, I imagine more than a few things were pilfered.'

'A few guns too,' said St. Just.

Guns. He let the word sit there between them for a moment before adding, 'You'll have heard by now what happened to the porter.'

'No. Which one?'

It was exactly the sort of answer St. Just would expect from an innocent person. He replied, 'Oliver Staunton.'

'Gosh. You're joking.'

'Not at all, sir.'

'I heard some commotion, but I haven't been outside my room today. I've been preparing for my supervision – waste of time, as it turns out.'

'No knowledge is ever wasted, sir.'

'I know what you think of me,' said Rufus with some spirit, 'but I am here to learn, as well as to enjoy myself. And I do take my work seriously. Anyway, I'm sorry about Oliver, but are you saying he was killed?'

'Yes. By a single bullet from a vintage weapon, still in working order.'

'A Luger, something from the war?'

'Exactly.'

'Lucky guess,' said Rufus. 'That's all, in case you're wondering. A lucky guess. But . . . what are you accusing me of? Should I get a lawyer? My family keeps an entire firm on retainer.'

'Oh, *gosh*, that sounds like a threat, sir,' said St. Just. But it didn't sound like balderdash. St. Just was sure Rufus was telling the truth about his team of lawyers, at least. 'But any lawyer worth his retainer will tell you that cooperating with us is the best path forward out of this . . . involvement of yours. I really am more interested in what your grandfather might've told you, for example, about stolen paintings.'

'I'm not sure what you mean. There was a famous Rembrandt retrieved, a self-portrait, and my grandfather was directly involved in saving that. It was a big day in his life. That was the one he couldn't stop talking about.'

'Just the one Rembrandt?'

Rufus sat back, clearly weighing his options. Truth or consequences. Finally he said,

'Look, this has nothing to do with me. And what I tell you
is only what I suspect – putting together the puzzle pieces,
you understand. My grandfather told me that a man was
working as a guard on the team and was left alone with some
of the finds that hadn't been catalogued or photographed yet.
And in my grandfather's memory, you see, there was a painting
there that had particularly caught his interest. But he was called
away – more likely went out for a smoke break; he always
smoked like a chimney – and when he returned, it was gone.
So was Rascallian.'

'Rascallian.'

'Yes, you heard right. His last name was Rascallian. My
grandfather said he saw him later that day, and he suspected
that in the intervening hours he had somehow hidden that
painting. Somewhere in a local village, in the hollow of a tree,
left with a friend – who knows? He accused him of it; the
man denied it.'

'And then time passes . . .'

'Right. Fast-forward decades, and who should I run across
but Sir Flyte Rascallian, Master of Hardwick College. An
unusual name. Obviously, of the wrong age to be the man my
grandfather suspected, but the right age to be his son or
something.'

'And you began looking into it?'

'I had just got here and had a lot of things to do, but yes,
I absolutely *planned* to look into it. Then that article appeared
in the paper. Then the master was killed. I never really got to
the bottom of it. Any more than the police seem to have done.
And now – two murders. I seem to be involved, and I don't
know how. But I no longer feel safe here at the college. I think
you'll find me next in private accommodation.'

'I would advise you not to leave the country,' said St. Just.
'But do keep us informed of your whereabouts.'

'You're forgetting my studies,' said Rufus. 'Of course I
can't just leave Cambridge. But I'll leave information with the
porters – if there are any left alive – about where you can
reach me. It will be through my lawyers.' His tone was

bordering on rude, and somehow implied this inconvenient move was all the police's fault. St. Just pretended to ignore the threat, but he knew enough of Rufus's background to realize he could mess up his investigation no end if he chose. The last thing his team needed was some high-priced solicitor or attorney making demands.

For now, St. Just decided to treat Rufus with kid gloves. He played the flattery card.

'You have information and skills that the police don't have, sir,' he said. 'And if you provide us with that information now, we will be happy to leave you in peace to find new lodgings.'

'What more do you need?'

'I was wondering if you had ever actually seen this purported Rembrandt. The painting that the master had in his possession.'

Rufus shifted uncomfortably, picking up a pillow from his bed and hugging it to himself. 'How in the world would I have seen that?' he said. 'Students aren't allowed in the master's quarters, not even graduate students like me.'

He began overexplaining, always a tell. Sergeant Fear scribbled down his words. St. Just wondered if what he said were strictly true. A student from a wealthy family might have been treated slightly differently, the hope being that some of their wealth might one day trickle back to the college in the form of scholarships or restoration efforts. A man in the master's position often played fund-raiser.

'I am in my first year, finding my feet,' Rufus went on. 'I only met him briefly when my year gathered initially. Seeing the painting? No, I mean really. You're reaching, Arthur – is it?'

'I'd rather we keep this on a formal basis. Anyway,' St. Just slapped his knees hard preparatory to standing. Rufus visibly jumped. 'I think that's all we can do for today, sir.'

'Good. Fine.'

'We appreciate your cooperation.'

'Think nothing of it. Hands across the water and all that.'

As they descended the stairs to Third Court, St. Just said, 'That's exactly what we'll do, think nothing of it. He's lying. His tell is shuffling his feet.'

'Also overexplaining,' said Fear. 'And hugging his pillow.'

'Right. I'm reminded how young he is. He wants to run from us. His brain says run, and he can't.'

'We're going to need more evidence than that, sir,' said Fear. 'Overexplaining, pillows, and restless feet.'

'I know. And I have an idea who to ask.'

TWENTY
My Funny Alibi

'You didn't ask Rufus about his alibi,' said Sergeant Fear as they made their way across First Court. The crime scene tape around the Porters' Lodge was intact, if a bit blown about by wind, although there was no police activity they could see. Serious Crime would be winding down operations now, the porter's body removed, the paperwork just begun.

'There was no need. I don't question that he had a solid alibi. It's been verified. The question is exactly why he needed one.'

'O-kaaay.'

'Where we went wrong,' said St. Just, 'was in suspecting Rufus as a killer just for establishing an alibi of any kind. We assumed he was up to no good – and as it turns out, that was true.

'But his alibi was not for murder. It was for something entirely different. Rufus is cold-blooded and calculating, yes, and capable of all manner of criminal behaviour, but he's not a murderer.'

'I always thought those were the exact qualities needed for a murderer,' said Fear. 'Maybe he's working his way up the ladder.'

'In this case he was up to no good, but again, he wasn't planning to kill the master. He was planning to steal from him.'

'You mean the Rembrandt?'

'Exactly,' said St. Just. 'Of course. The Rembrandt.'

'But when would he ever have had the chance to even see it? To even know for certain the master had such a thing? I tend to believe him on that score, guv. Sir Flyte wasn't his mentor, that's been established. Rufus wouldn't have had access to his study for a supervision or even a chat.'

'Rufus wanted the master as his guide, of course, but that

wasn't going to happen. Poor Rufus was stuck with the Old Bailey for his tutes. But the master noticed Rufus right away, no doubt. Rufus has that quality. And perhaps the master made a mental note to keep an eye on him.'

'You don't mean . . .'

'No, nothing like that. There was never a whiff of scandal in the master's relationships with his charges. Everything about him was quite proper and above board. But once Sir Flyte saw Rufus's interest in Peyton, realizing the kind of man Rufus was, he couldn't *not* intervene. The key to the master's personality was a highly developed sense of family. It led to his downfall, in fact. His loyalty to Peyton.'

'To Peyton?'

'Loyalty, protectiveness. Family feeling may run higher in some people than in others. But I was thinking just now of his uncle.'

'What?'

'I'll get to that in a moment. Yes, he must have seen Rufus with Peyton – she was often visiting Rufus at the college – and I think the master was alarmed. Anyone spending five minutes in Rufus's company might have reservations as to his probity. He was clearly an ambitious young man but beyond normal ambition, a man with an eye for the main chance. The master was horrified to realize that Peyton was involved with him. And once he learned Peyton was his daughter, it brought out some latent instinct of protectiveness and – let's call it what it was – love.'

'How do you know for certain she was his daughter?'

'Partly from his reaction to that painting he saw in a museum with Annalise Bellagamba. But more than that, in that briefcase full of papers he inherited from his aunt. You haven't gone through the entire email yet, have you? I had a quick read-through earlier.'

'And that's how the master found out Peyton was his daughter? What was it, an ancestry kit?'

'Exactly. There was a match online when his aunt uploaded her and his uncle's DNA. Unless you hide your profile, it's there for any client of the service to see, although you can use just your initials or some pseudonym. His uncle's direct lineage included a girl named Peyton, who used her full name when she used the service. But she was not his daughter, she was his great-niece.'

'I see,' said Fear slowly. 'And putting two and two together . . . I see. So Sir Flyte tried to talk to Rufus. Maybe discourage him from hanging around his daughter?'

'I think that's exactly what he did. All very Victorian, of course, and doomed to failure. No one tells Rufus what to do. I don't think anyone told Peyton what to do either. In that respect, they were made for each other. In that and other respects.'

'How do you mean?'

'I mean Rufus used Peyton to get what he wanted, and she went along with it. She could always have refused to become involved in anything shady, but she went along. She was that besotted with him. I remember her saying something to the effect she couldn't wait to be in New York with him. And you saw the way her eyes would light up talking about him. I think she had an entire fantasy built up around living with Rufus in America. Married, for preference. How much he fed that fantasy is anyone's guess. He probably said exactly what she wanted to hear to get what he wanted. He's playing a very old game in many ways.'

'So she was his alibi?'

'No. She did the dirty work for him so he would have an unbreakable alibi from scores of other people.'

'Wait. You're saying Peyton stole the painting?'

'That's to be determined, but I think that was the game. Until we find the painting, or she confesses, we can't know for sure. But Rufus's alibi was watertight – suspiciously so. He went out of his way to be noticed, to be filmed, to upload videos and so on to social media and have others do the same. We could see how unbreakable it all was, and how we had no choice but to eliminate him as a suspect. We never guessed that he was using Peyton to get away with another crime. A crime for which she'd never be suspected.'

'Wait. First let me get this straight, about the Rembrandt: you think the master called Rufus into his study to read him the riot act, and that's when Rufus saw the painting?'

'I would imagine cajoling and persuasion and perhaps a veiled threat or two would've been the master's technique before he went for the riot act. But, yes, that's what I'm thinking.'

'And when Rufus was in the office, he saw the Rembrandt,' Fear said.

'Yes. I gathered from what Ambrose told us that the painting was mingled with other paintings from the collection he got from his aunt. The master may have decided some version of hiding it in plain sight was best, like in Poe's *The Purloined Letter*. But Rufus saw it. Perhaps the master left him alone in his study for a moment, and Rufus took the opportunity to rifle through the stacks of paintings. I wonder if we couldn't find his prints somewhere in the room, and thereby prove the lie he was never in that study.'

'But softly, softly, or he *will* call his team of lawyers.'

'He'll need to eventually if I'm right about this. We must remember, putting aside his questionable ethics, that Rufus was an art historian from a highly respected university in the United States. He was here as a graduate student of art history. If he saw that painting, he knew exactly what he was looking at.'

'All right . . . I guess.'

'It makes even more sense when you realize he already knew the painting. He recognized it because he had read a description of it. Or had heard of it.'

'Where?'

'In a list of paintings that went missing during the Holocaust, presumed stolen or destroyed. Paintings and other art objects that remain unaccounted for. And perhaps . . . perhaps from a more direct source.'

'You're not serious. Wouldn't the master have spotted it, as well?'

'The master did. I'm sure of it.'

TWENTY-ONE
Zooming In

The connection was remarkably clear. St. Just could never quite wrap his head round the fact that he could talk to and, moreover, *see* someone at the other end of a videoconference link – someone who was practically a world away.

It was still daylight in New York in the States, and he had had no trouble raising the party he wanted to speak to.

The woman who appeared on the screen was perhaps forty-five, with a bouffant hairstyle and dark-framed glasses that did not quite hide the beauty of her molten brown eyes. St. Just wondered at the choice, but it wasn't his place to comment on new fashion. She introduced herself as Moira Hensley and explained that Mr Franklin Penn would join them soon.

She turned off the microphone while she shuffled paperwork, waiting until Mr Penn appeared. Meanwhile, St. Just and Sergeant Fear held a muted, sidebar discussion.

Fear said, 'The information Henderson found in army archives is that Sir Flyte's uncle was indeed assigned to duty in Germany, at one point guarding the Monuments Men. This is not to say we can pin this on Finneas Rascallian, but really, what are the chances? What may be a true Rembrandt painting ended up in his attic after all.'

'I don't see any problem making the connection. But I need to hear it from the man himself, who may have been a witness to a crime so many years ago. Look, here he is.'

A little square appeared on the screen next to Moira's face. At a verbal command from Mr Penn, which they could not hear, and a dismissive wave of a freckled, gnarled hand, the square containing Moira vanished and the microphone beneath Mr Penn's square turned green to indicate a live mic. They were left talking to the titan of industry himself, Mr Franklin Penn.

'Hello, sir, thank you for taking the time to speak with us today,' said St. Just.

'You had me at Rembrandt, Inspector.' Behind him, the two policemen could see what looked to be mahogany panelling hung with dozens of paintings of every size. 'Ask me anything. What is it you want to know?'

'Have you spoken to your grandson recently?'

If the question surprised him, he hid it well. 'Oh, I wish,' said Mr Penn. 'I told him when he went over there that he shouldn't waste a moment calling his boring old grandfather. He should be out there enjoying himself. But the truth is I'm dying to know everything he's up to.

'You know, I was at Cambridge myself. Different world. I wish I'd been there at the time of the Cambridge spies. They don't seem to be able to decide if there were five or six of them, but it has spawned an entire industry. Anthony Blunt – up to no good, I spotted it later, but no one asked me. Superior sort, you know. Thought he was smarter than everyone else. I guess in a way he was – he got away with it for so long.'

St. Just was tempted to wander down that alley. The Cambridge spies were a particular passion of his, and the topic seemed inexhaustible. No one could understand why the young sons of privilege had turned their backs so thoroughly on lives of which others could only dream.

But today they were on a different quest.

'You were with the Monuments Men?' St. Just asked the wizened face on the screen. Two small round lights were reflected in his glasses from some sort of lighting enhancement gadget that St. Just had seen advertised, but the most professional lighting couldn't hide the fact that Franklin Penn looked to be about a thousand years old. It was one of God's miracles he was still around to talk with him, and that this technology allowed it without the need for travel on either side. Even flying on a private jet, it was doubtful Mr Penn would have survived the trip.

'Indeed.'

Penn spoke in a raspy voice; it was like listening to the hum of an air purifier. St. Just leaned in as Sergeant Fear turned up the volume on the computer.

'You see, my older brother spent most of his time at the start of the war in a French farmhouse, hiding out. He was spotted jumping out of a plane, and his priority became getting his shattered leg in good enough shape for him hightail it into Spain. He always felt thwarted by the accident, you know. He wanted to fight in what we both knew was a just cause. So, when there was a chance for me to go, I jumped at it. With my background and a few connections, I was quickly integrated into the Monuments Men.'

'And where did the job take you?'

'Oh, everywhere. Everywhere! Initially we focused on saving churches, palaces, structural things like that, but we ended up looking for artworks hidden by the Nazis. I was in Paris, then Germany, where the Heilbronn and Kochendorf mines yielded their treasures.'

He was overtaken with a prolonged cough, and they waited patiently.

'We had good intel, which made it all possible. You see, we were under the gun timewise. We feared the Germans might destroy anything the Allies might want. We had to keep one step ahead of them. Mostly we succeeded. But in a way, we were wrong about their intentions, at least until it all went to hell for them. Hitler wanted to preserve everything – everything he didn't consider degenerate – to build his museum in Austria.'

'Were you at Neuschwanstein Castle?'

'Of course. For the outline of the story, I would refer you to the movie. It mostly got it right. I've watched it a few times and I still tear up at the scenes with the Ghent altarpiece and the Michelangelo. But there were over twenty thousand items in Neuschwanstein alone. I can still see the beauty . . . the glint of gold.

'We rescued so many objects. Millions. The scene was chaos. Mines and caves. That's why . . . You see, there was so much to take in, so much to account for.'

'And there was a Rembrandt?'

'The scene was chaotic,' he repeated. 'Paintings, statues, altarpieces all over the place. You have to wonder why Hitler would care about religious art. It makes no—'

'The Rembrandt?' St. Just prodded.

'Among all that, yes, I remember well seeing the self-portrait of Rembrandt. That was at Heilbronn. I wouldn't mistake it for anything else. It was authentic. And there was another, a smaller one, that was almost certainly his.

'But once the self-portrait had been secured, I made the error of trusting others to guard the rest. I left on a call of nature, and when I returned and looked for it later, the smaller painting was gone. I'm not sure anyone believed me. How could they? I was the only one who had seen it. We're talking about the portrait of a young woman, right?'

St. Just struggled to follow him. 'Yes. The young woman. You say you saw it?'

'That is what I'm saying, isn't it? Are you deaf, man? No matter what you may be thinking, my memory is as sharp as it ever has been. I can call that picture up before my mind in *every* detail. I had a photographic memory then and now. It's a trait I passed along to my grandson.'

'A portrait of a young woman.'

'Yes, it was there, and then it was gone. I was gutted, let me tell you. You know that old question: "If the Louvre was on fire, would you rescue the art or the people?" I'm afraid I always had trouble answering that one. A character flaw, no doubt. My grandson has no hesitation. He thinks people are replaceable. I've failed him, I guess.'

Franklin Penn was silent for so long that they thought the connection had dropped. He and Fear exchanged glances. Had he fallen asleep?

Sergeant Fear said, 'Sir? Mr Penn?' Still no answer.

'And the self-portrait remained?' St. Just prompted at last, rather loudly. He had begun to doubt the old man's memory of events. Surely he had some facts mixed up?

'Yes, yes,' he said at last, his voice still a raspy murmur. 'No need to shout. It was a portrait of a young woman that disappeared, no doubt one of his mistresses. He did a lot of those, Rembrandt. He liked using his lady friends as models.

Saved money that way. He had quite a colourful private life, especially after his wife died. Her family came after him for money and jewellery but he'd given it away . . . I forget now . . . gave it to his son so they couldn't get their paws on it. He died poor, did you know that? He never knew . . .' He stopped to draw a ragged breath. 'He never knew how great he would become, how revered. Can you imagine? So sad . . .'

St. Just felt he was losing him to Rembrandt's life story and needed to draw the conversation back along more urgent lines.

'So, who was left in charge of guarding this treasure? There must have been more than one man.'

'Oh, yes, a dozen or so. Most were outside by this time, celebrating. It was just this fizz of excitement. Up until then, most of us had been on our own, or maybe with one other person. Not a big platoon, like in the movie. So many irre-placeable items, and we had saved the day. But I was certain someone was there for himself. Out for his own purposes, was Rascallian.'

'Finneas Rascallian,' St. Just supplied. 'You're suggesting he took the painting of the young woman?'

'I would bet any money on it.'

'Did you report it?'

'Of course. I can have my wife send you the report if you'd like.' He turned to look over his shoulder. 'Moira, is the fax machine working?'

'We got rid of that years ago, dear. It's all email now.'

St. Just could read Fear's expression without needing to look: *Wife?*

'It would be most helpful if you could email us copies,' said St. Just.

'Where they went wrong, you see,' Franklin Penn continued, 'was when they found the Rembrandt self-portrait mixed in with lesser artwork. I say lesser, but relative to a Rembrandt or a Michelangelo, nearly everything is lesser, isn't it? Anyway, in the excitement, the inventory reflected only one Rembrandt. But there were two. I could never get anyone to add that to the official tally, not at the time, because it made it clear that if the painting had been there and was now gone, we didn't

just have the Nazi thieves to deal with, but we had a thief
among our own men. It would have been a huge embarrassment
and our mission was so vital, so prestigious. So . . .'

'So they covered it up,' St. Just finished for him.

'They didn't believe me, they said. But yes, it was a cover-up
– no more and no less. It happens all the time in the art world.
Well, not just in the art world. When a bank gets its data
hacked, do they run around announcing it? Not unless they
have no choice.

'And when an art gallery is in charge of precious artifacts,
and it turns out there's a thief at work in the basement hoarding
treasure for himself, or herself, they don't want to advertise
how careless they've been.'

'And that's what you think happened here?'

'I didn't have seniority,' he said. 'I was the youngest of the
bunch – most of these guys were older, seasoned experts. I
had no seniority at all, no authority, so I doubted I'd be believed.
They treated me like a younger brother, and a stupid one at
that, which was outrageous. I knew as much as the lot of
them.'

He paused, adding, 'It was probably the first time in my
life my family's fortune didn't help me get my way. We were
a team, working for the common good, and I was just a cog
in the wheel. I was simply the young guy – the rich kid – who
knew something about paintings and because of my mother I
could speak German. It was a real comeuppance for me, and
I never forgot the lesson. I remember . . .'

He then launched into a long reminiscence of his activities
after the great find, the end of the mopping-up activities, the
return home, his being awarded the Congressional Medal of
Honor. St. Just disliked interrupting him, but it was necessary
to act quickly on what Penn had told them. Just as he was
getting ready to sign off as politely as he could, Moira appeared
behind him and took control.

'Evelyn called,' she said to her husband. To the policemen
she said, 'I'm afraid Mr Penn has another call. We have to let
you go now.'

And without further ado, they both disappeared from the
screen.

'He was a bit erratic, wasn't he?' Fear observed, once he was sure the connection had ended. 'Mostly there, then not. My grandfather was the same at the end, such an old tortoise. Perfectly lucid stories, followed by moments of weird silence. He'd tell you three times what he had for lunch. But overall, I'd say when Penn is talking about this young woman's portrait, this Rembrandt, his memory is clear.'

'I'd agree.'

'So, we have a sort of chain of possession? A stolen artwork, found hidden in Germany, ends up in England in the attic of a man named Finneas Rascallian. He dies and leaves all his possessions to his wife, who then dies and leaves everything to the nephew. Sir Flyte Rascallian.'

'In the end,' St. Just mused, 'only Sir Flyte knew – or at least strongly suspected – what he had been bequeathed. But how to explain having it? Even with his aunt and uncle dead, it was an embarrassment that could only be addressed head on, with the truth. It was a stolen painting. Plundered.'

'No doubt originally taken from some terrified owner under duress.'

'Indeed. Perhaps he was working up his courage to return it to the people in charge of reparations. But with his love of Rembrandt, his *obsession*, wouldn't he have wanted to possess it just a little bit longer? Look at it a bit longer? Study it? Which surely is why he kept it in his office. So he could stare at it for hours on end. He might have told himself, "What difference does it make? It's been so many years. I'll get around to it. There's plenty of time."'

'And then, of course, there was not time – not for him. And the painting is still missing,' Fear added.

'I wonder . . .'

'What, guv?'

'The first time we interviewed Rufus Penn, his room was a tip, wasn't it?'

'Yes.'

'And it was even worse when we visited him today.'

'Yes. And?'

'I'm thinking again of that story where something valuable is hidden in plain sight. *The Purloined Letter*. If I were looking to hide a painting, I wouldn't leave it in a safe that could be broken into. I'd leave it where it could be overlooked, where it blended in, where it wouldn't be found until I was ready to retrieve it.'

'I don't follow.'

'I'm not sure . . . But it's time to talk to Peyton again. I think she has the answers we're looking for.'

In that, as things turned out, he was wrong, but only slightly.

TWENTY-TWO
Peyton's Place

S t. Just had been hoping for a little more privacy, but a noisy wedding party was gathered in the main room at Virtue.

Still, the interview couldn't wait. As the day wore on and more customers arrived, the conversation would only become more uncomfortable.

Not for him, but for Peyton Beadle-Batsford.

She still seemed to be playing dual roles of hostess and waitress. Not quite yet the sous chef position she wanted, but it was undoubtedly a steady job in such a popular spot. He wondered how quickly she would leave it to follow Rufus once his one-year course was up. He suspected, very quickly indeed.

Maybe he would stay on for a PhD, giving her time and space to see him more clearly. If she were both lucky and wise.

But St. Just did not see Peyton as a particularly wise young woman.

Minutes ago, he and Fear had been sitting in the car outside the restaurant looking closely at email images of fingerprints found in Sir Flyte's study and comparing them with the prints taken from St. Just's credit card. To the naked eye, Peyton's prints were an exact match to many of the prints found at the scene. The others were likely visitors and bedders and were still being eliminated. Rufus's prints might well be among them. Perhaps Rufus would cooperate in offering comparison prints, although he'd no doubt throw up a wall of solicitors to stall the process.

Of course, none of this would stand up in court. A barrister would certainly question the means of collecting Peyton's prints. For St. Just's purposes, the crucial issue was whether

Peyton had been in the master's room. She had denied it. The question was why. Why lie to the police? The range of excuses spanned from the criminal to the potentially embarrassing. This interview was intended for St. Just and Fear to find out.

'Do you have somewhere we could talk?' he asked Peyton. 'Perhaps a room for private parties? Because, I'm afraid, the conversation might be awkward this time, and you might want some privacy.'

'This really couldn't come at a worse moment,' she began. 'There's this wedding, and—'

'I am aware of that,' he said. 'Find someone to cover for you for fifteen minutes. It's not optional, Ms Beadle-Batsford. It's here or down at the station. Your choice.'

He studied her face for signs that she could anticipate the topic. All he saw, though, was confusion and a spark of annoyance.

'Very well,' she said. 'Follow me.'

She led them to a room near the back, away from the kitchen. It didn't have a private door, but it was remote enough to suit their purpose.

He got right to the point.

'You told us you had never been in the Master's Lodge.'

'That's right,' she said. Sergeant Fear rather showily made a note of the denial.

'Unfortunately, we have evidence you were there. It would behove you to tell us, now, everything you know. If I must get a warrant for your fingerprints and DNA, I will. But I'd much prefer that you simply be straight with me. There's been a lot of nonsense, all of it criminal, but nothing reaching the level of murder. My chief thinks you fit the bill for the murder, and I'm not sure I'll be able to hold him off.'

'But I don't . . . It's not . . .'

'Before you say you don't know what I'm talking about, let me tell you what I *think* you were doing in the Master's Lodge, in his study, on the night he died. Because there's no question you were there. And since you're no longer a member of the college, there's absolutely no reason you should so recently be in the Master's Lodge, leaving fresh prints behind. It was rather foolish of you not to take such a basic precaution as to wear gloves. But I don't think you're a hardened criminal. It never occurred to you to use gloves because they might've got in your way as you navigated across the roof, down through the attic, the stairs, and into his study. Your prints are everywhere in that room. We are talking murder, Ms Beadle-Batsford.'

She looked completely crestfallen now. The mention of a murder charge had had the desired effect.

'He was dead when I got there,' she said. 'I swear it. And I've never been so frightened in my life.'

'What time are we talking about?'

'I was there at midnight. I don't know what time he was killed because I had nothing to do with it. You must believe me; I would never hurt him, or anyone for that matter. He was dead when I got there. It scared the hell out of me, and without even knowing it, I screamed. Then I realized that would alert the porter so I had to leave quickly.'

'But only after having a quick look round for the Rembrandt.'

'I know it looks bad, but that was why I was there. I knew it would take the porter a few minutes to get there, he could barely walk, so . . .'

'We found your prints on many paintings,' said St. Just, 'in precisely the upper back position someone would use when rifling through a stack of paintings against a wall. The Rembrandt – was it there?'

'There were all sorts of paintings, but I would swear, nothing that looked like a Rembrandt.'

'To be clear, we're talking about a small, framed painting of a young girl or woman?'

'Yes.'

'And what possessed you,' said St. Just, 'to break into the Master's Lodge and look for such a painting? Were you planning to fence it?'

'Hardly,' she replied, allowing herself a tinge of sarcasm. 'If there are fences for stolen art in Cambridge, which I'm sure there are, I wouldn't know them.'

'So you were stealing the painting for someone else, is that right?'

'Um. I wouldn't say "stealing".'

'I would.'

She wouldn't meet his eyes, and he gave her a moment to collect her thoughts. Then he pounced. 'Rufus.' Just the one word.

'It wasn't *stealing*,' she insisted. 'It didn't belong to the master. It belonged to whoever it was stolen from, and we were going to return it to the proper owner.'

St. Just sighed. Oh, to be young! He kept forgetting how young she was.

'I thought it was something like that,' he said. 'That's all very noble and idealistic, but whoever wanted the master dead, whoever was willing to kill him over a painting, did not have such noble motives. Surely you can see that. And surely you can see also that you're deeply involved in something that, to be honest, could have ended your life.'

'I don't see how *that* can be true,' she said.

'You're implicated in something far above your age and background and abilities to handle, involving at least one very unsavoury character. Did you see anything when you were in the room?'

'Apart from the master?' She shook her head, as if to free it of the memory.

'That's what I meant, yes. Apart from the master's body.'

'You mean someone hiding in the shadows or something like that? No, whoever had killed him was long gone. And no doubt taken the painting with them. The room didn't have any hiding places or closets, no hangings to hide behind, that sort of thing. Just those mullioned windows with no curtains. I took a quick look round, and that was all I could do. Then I had to leave because someone, probably the porter, would be on their way. I had screamed pretty loudly. The carriage clock in the study going off, the bell in the chapel tower striking midnight – it unnerved me. I really screwed up.'

How strange she would see it that way, although he understood what she meant. If the point had been not to get caught, she'd had a narrow escape all round. Also, possibly, from a murder charge.

'So, where do we go from here?' asked Peyton. 'Am I being arrested?'

'I think that rather depends on your telling me and my sergeant here the whole truth. You're not being forced to talk to us, but it would be a very good idea if, in fact, you care about who murdered the master and can convince us it wasn't you.'

'I've told you all I know,' she said.

'Let me be the judge of that.'

'Oh, judge and jury, are we now?' But the stuffing had gone out of her. She was smart enough to see the consequences, and that St. Just might be trying to hand her a lifeline.

'Walk me through that night,' he said. 'You had the dinner party at your mother's house. Perhaps you did the washing-up alone or with her – it doesn't matter.' *Or does it?* A thought began to circle his mind. 'But once she had gone to bed, you sneaked out of the house.'

'I didn't sneak. It was my house, and I'm an adult.'

'You left the house to keep a prearranged appointment. Let me tell you what I think happened. You let yourself into Rufus's staircase, which is generally unlocked. He had given you a copy of the keys to both that staircase and to his rooms, which you would need if your mission was successful. You took the stairs to the door of the roof, and from there, you walked across the rooftops – crawling where needed, to avoid being observed – and made your way over to the roof of the Master's Lodge. This wasn't your first expedition over there, was it?'

'It was, actually. Rufus had done a reconnoitre and let me know what the layout was. He took some video. It was super simple. There was no lock on the lodge's access door to the attic. I simply climbed in, made my way through the attic, and then down the stairs of the lodge. I was expecting the master to be asleep at that time of night. So, I tiptoed past what I thought must be his bedroom and headed for his study. Rufus had told me the painting was sure to be in his study.'

'You didn't hear anyone else in the house?'

'No, and believe me, I was on high alert. If the master had woken up, I would've had a lot of explaining to do, and I'd be in a world of trouble, I knew that, but as it turned out . . .'

'You needn't have worried. He was dead and not overhearing anything.'

'Yes, I saw him there at his desk. It was obvious there was no hope of saving him, of helping. It was midnight, and as the chapel bell tolled the hour, I just lost it and let out a tremendous scream – that was a mistake. The first real mistake I made.'

'Apart from the mistake of being there in the first place?'

'OK, fine, yes, it was a mistake being there. But I looked around; I could not find the painting.'

'The one Rufus had described to you?'

'Yes, the one he described to me. He was very specific. But there was nothing even close to that. Everything else was wrong century, wrong artist.'

'Let's say you did find the painting. What were you meant to do?'

She answered readily. 'I was to take it to Rufus. He would make sure it made its way to the proper owner. He had done research on it and said it had been stolen from a Jewish family in Germany. There were all kinds of documents attesting to the provenance and there are organizations dedicated to making reparations – returning the stolen works, generally to descendants of the people they were stolen from.'

'And how did Rufus plan to explain how this painting came into his possession?'

'I think he was planning to wait until his grandfather died, which would be any minute, honestly. He's quite old.'

'I'm sorry, what? Why did the grandfather have anything to do with this?'

'Rufus was going to claim that it came from his grandfather.'

'Oh.' St. Just was appalled. 'He was going to drag that old man's reputation through the mud? Claim he'd stolen it while he worked with the Monuments Men?'

'It's not as if he'd know.'

'That's not the point, Ms Beadle-Batsford. That is simply not the point.' St. Just was beginning to think Peyton and Rufus were made for each other, after all.

'Well, he could hardly say that I stole it for him.'

'I think that is entirely naïve on your part. I believe that's exactly what he planned to do if push came to shove.'

'Rufus loves me. He would never do that to me.'

St. Just sighed. 'Be that as it may, you say the painting wasn't there.'

'I swear on my mother's life, I am telling you the truth. It wasn't there.'

St. Just and Sergeant Fear made their way out of the restaurant, passing a screeching bride and a clearly inebriated groom. All the bridesmaids were wearing too-fussy frocks of gold and purple cloth. Their elaborate updos had been caught in the rain and they looked the worse for wear, but no one seemed to mind.

Once outside, Sergeant Fear turned to St. Just and said, 'So, where is the painting?'

'Are we quite certain that the home and gallery of the curator, Ambrose Nussknacker, were thoroughly searched?'

'Yes, according to Henderson, and he said Nussknacker was completely cooperative. He had an "I have nothing to hide" attitude. He stayed with the team as they went through every inch of the place, photographing all the artwork. But there was nothing resembling a painting of a young girl by an Old Master. In fact, Henderson said most of it was modern-day work mixed with old clay pots and coins from some excavation or other. Dull stuff, he called it. I don't suppose many people can afford a Rembrandt for their galleries.'

'Or be able to afford the security and insurance to display it.'

'No.'

'All right. I think it's clear that Rufus was involved beyond what Peyton indicates, keeping in mind that he engineered this whole night-climbing escapade. Also remembering that the master had Rufus's number. Sir Flyte knew the painting would be of great interest to Rufus, especially given his · heritage. Perhaps the master called Rufus into his lodgings on that pretext but in fact to try to warn him off Peyton.

'The master realized the painting needed to be hidden to prevent it from being stolen, especially after that newspaper article by Barnard LaFarge came out on the *Bugle*'s website. He couldn't keep it in the Master's Lodge any longer, much as he may have wanted to. I've been wondering if he might have entrusted it to the porter. If we're missing the obvious: that Oliver was in on this to the extent that he was given a parcel by the master, told to guard it with his life, and that's exactly what he did. That's exactly what a loyal man like Oliver would do. But we've searched the Porters' Lodge for it, too.'

'Of course, we searched it as a crime scene,' said Fear. 'It wasn't ransacked, but there were indications someone had gone through it – the day porter said she thought a few things on the shelves were out of order, but she wasn't certain. Our own search turned up nothing suspicious, and nothing that looked like artwork. Just poor Oliver, sitting there dead, quite alone.'

'But, what about Oliver's grandson? Gerry? What if he saw the article in the paper?'

'It's a stretch. How would he know Oliver had the painting for safekeeping? *If* he did?'

'Would Oliver have trusted his grandson with it, or told him he was holding it for the master? He didn't seem to have any sense of who or what his grandson was.'

'Perhaps . . .'

'No,' said St. Just. 'On second thoughts, I don't think that works. He would've known or feared Gerry would sell it on for drugs. He wouldn't like facing the truth, but I don't see him breaking his word to the master to guard the thing well. He was far too dutiful for that.'

'I believe you're right. That sounds right.'

'There's another possibility. But it doesn't put the master in the best light.'

'What's that?'

'He hid the painting in a place where, if it were found, it would make someone look very bad indeed. It might get that person in trouble. If the painting weren't found, well, the master had gained a bit of breathing space while he decided what to do with it. His preference might've been that it would just disappear altogether, but it was a famous and no doubt beautiful artifact, and I'm quite certain he couldn't bring himself to destroy it. But in the meantime, he knew it couldn't stay in his lodge.'

'Where would he put it?' Fear asked. 'He would not have had time to put it in the bank in a safety deposit box, would he?'

'We've already rung his bank, remember? He never accessed his safety deposit box in the time between his aunt's death and his own, and besides, the box wasn't large enough to hold even a small painting in a frame.'

'So what would he do with it?'

'There is one more place we might look. I hope I'm wrong about this, but I'm sure the master would tell himself it was only temporary, and no harm done.'

'Are you going to tell me what you mean?'

'In his last days, what was preoccupying the master? The masterpiece he'd inherited, and his desire to protect the family name from his uncle's actions, yes. But overriding that, and mixed in with that, was his concern for Peyton. His desire to get her out of Rufus's clutches.'

'Yes. Are you sure she's his daughter?'

'He had the paperwork to prove it, in that briefcase he inherited from his aunt. It's the only thing that explains his interest in Peyton, his standing up for her. She wasn't even a member of the college anymore.'

'I see,' said Fear. 'Yes, I think I see.'

'Imagine a man nearing the end of his life, quite alone in the world. Lauded for his work, a huge success in that regard, but with no wife or family or close friends outside of work. And then one day he learns Peyton is his. That he's helped create this lovely young life.'

'And he confirmed this . . . how?'

'Let's go and ask her mother that question.'

TWENTY-THREE
The Family That Lies Together

'I don't see what business this is of yours,' said Patricia Beadle-Batsford. 'If I had thought it was police business, I would've told you.'

'We rather wish you had,' said St. Just.

They were in the sitting room of the professor's house. When St. Just had rung her mobile, she had explained she was working from home that day and had tried to avoid the interview using business as an excuse.

Working from home wasn't often an option for a policeman, but it remained a common phenomenon elsewhere since the pandemic. Portia often worked from her home office, holding Zoom supervisions. If she also worked on one of her crime novels here and there, who was to know? She never missed a beat on either count.

'I realize these are your working hours, and I appreciate your taking the time once again to talk to us,' he said. 'But surely you see that your daughter's connection to the master is a key element of the case.'

'I don't see why it would be.'

'Don't you? In our line of work, inheritance often comes to the fore, and killing for gain is often a motive. We see it all the time.'

She sat in stunned silence for a moment before replying. 'Surely you're not suggesting Peyton . . .?'

'I suggest nothing except we would've fumbled around in the dark for a much shorter time had you come forward and been completely honest with us.'

'So you could accuse my daughter of murder? Is that your game? Really?'

She sat upright on the couch, her arms tight across her chest. St. Just's eyes sought out any resemblance to the painting

Annalise Bellagamba had told them about, the painting of
Bathsheba that the master had been so taken with. The signs
were there, he realized. Patricia's body was far thinner, her
face lined with age and etched with the discord of her personality. But the likeness was there in a more youthful form, if
you chose to look.

Everything in her demeanour now suggested she was frozen
in place, for she was too sensible a person to try to flee. But
the lies of twenty years had finally caught up with her, leaving
her almost literally petrified.

As he waited for her to continue, he became aware of the
scent of burning wood from the fire.

'How did you find out?' she managed at last.

'We have our ways,' he said. He had been going on hints
that the master, through his over protective actions, had
provided, and a search of the UK birth records had further
confirmed the DNA test results. Flyte Rascallian was named
quite openly on Peyton's birth certificate as her father. Whether
he had ever acknowledged or even known about the birth at
the time, it was something that couldn't have been kept secret
much longer.

All Peyton had to do was ask for a passport one day, say
for a trip to America with Rufus, and the game would be up.
Her mother must've realized this. Perhaps she unknowingly
had aligned with the master in wanting to break up the relationship, and for similar reasons. Maybe she also saw Rufus
as bad news: rich, handsome, surely using her daughter, and
nothing but trouble. And she'd been hoping the day he was
exposed for what he was would not be far off.

Although, was his exposure really necessary? Rufus would
break it off with her daughter without a backward glance as
soon as she became inconvenient, which seemed to be
happening very quickly indeed.

'You're wondering why I didn't tell her, aren't you? If it's
any of your business – which I maintain it is not – it just sort
of . . . happened. My silence. The longer I didn't tell my
daughter, the harder it got to tell her. There was a moment
when she was thirteen, and she and I had a fight over something – something trivial. We often fought in those days. She

reminded me so much of Flyte – stubborn, you know; opin-
ionated, always right. I nearly told her then. But I would have
been doing it out of . . . I don't know. Out of spite, I guess.
To hurt her. And everything else aside, I would never hurt my
daughter or want to see her hurt.'

St. Just knew this was true. He also wondered how far she
would go to save Peyton from harm.

'Listen, Professor,' said St. Just. 'We don't seem to have
got off on the best footing here. I don't have any reason to
believe right now that your daughter killed Flyte, nor that she
would want to. But it can't be forgotten that he had recently
inherited a painting potentially worth many millions of dollars.
Provided that painting belonged to him legally – and for all
anyone knew, it did – she would inherit at his death, as his
legal heir. As his only heir. There seems to have been no one
else.'

She laughed briefly – a joyless laugh. 'Yes, you can include
me in that. I was not married to him, as I'm sure you know.
He wasn't having any of that. It really was the briefest fling
imaginable and, to be completely clear, my philosophy does
not include tying myself to any man for life.'

'But you named him on the birth certificate.'

'I wish I hadn't now, but at the time, I saw no reason to lie.'

Except to your daughter, who has a vested interest in
knowing, St. Just thought.

'Are you aware that Peyton left the house that night? The
night of Sir Flyte's murder?'

Her tone was flat. 'No.' She seemed to rally, adding,
'Furthermore, I think that's an extraordinary accusation. I
believe this has gone far enough. Ask Ambrose, if you must.
He came back here, later that night. He can tell you.'

'You're just telling us this now?'

'We are all innocent! There was no need to overexplain our
actions, to answer questions that weren't asked.'

'Professor, you are being disingenuous, and you know it.
You deliberately failed to mention Ambrose's return here.
Why?'

'I thought you – I thought it would just go away. It had
nothing to do with us.'

Before she could invoke a solicitor, St. Just interjected, 'We have Peyton's own admission.'

'No, you don't. You can't. You've coerced her, a young girl – I know how these things work.'

'Look here,' said St. Just. 'She doesn't admit to murder, and to be honest, I don't think she's capable of it. But she does say that she left the house that night and she is a little more involved in this than you may have been led to believe. You may indeed want to get a solicitor for her.' *And for your-self*, he did not add. 'But again, we're not charging her with anything right now. We need to find the murderer of two men. If you can't tell us anything about that . . .' He left the sentence open in the quiet room, waiting, giving her time to respond. He hadn't abandoned the idea that Patricia herself might be the guilty party.

'I will be contacting my solicitor,' she said. 'And I think you had better leave now.'

Perhaps we better had, thought St. Just. If Professor Patricia Beadle-Batsford were indeed the killer, he would need to be careful from this point forward to dot all the I's and cross all the T's for the prosecution. The mention of a solicitor, which he had in fact hoped to avoid for quite a while longer, forced him to retreat, if only momentarily.

There were other ways of getting to the truth.

TWENTY-FOUR
The Action of Untying

'Do you think she did it?' Sergeant Fear asked as they climbed back into the car.

'It's a working theory,' said St. Just. 'Just one of several I've been turning over in my mind. But I think we've suspected all along who did it.'

Fear knew from experience that the 'we' was mere politeness on St. Just's part. The truth was Fear didn't have a clue. Then the last part of what St. Just had said landed.

'Do not tell me you knew all along,' he said. This was just like claiming to have known whodunnit from the first chapter of a murder mystery. It was no more than simple showing off. He held St. Just in higher esteem.

'All along?' said St. Just. 'Of course not. This case had many suspects, and we had to eliminate them all. I still like the mother for this, but frankly, if she were looking for revenge over Sir Flyte after all these years, the woman-scorned motivation just doesn't fit – not the timeline, and not her personality.'

'So who?'

'Ambrose Nussknacker. Of course.'

Fear didn't think that 'of course' was strictly necessary, but wisely he held his tongue.

'Ambrose Nussknacker was an alumnus of Hardwick College, did you know? That was not something he mentioned to us – and why should he? – but the information was accessible online. And it was evident from the beginning that whoever did this was familiar with the college and its routines.'

'That could be almost any of them,' said Fear, but that sounded very close to being a sour grapes response, so he said no more. 'Besides, as we just learned, the professor alibis him for the master's murder.'

'Does she?' St. Just asked. 'Does she really? Think about that.'

Sergeant Fear thought, but to no avail. 'Go on.'

'Now, Ambrose had graduated some years before from Hardwick College, but it was because of his business relationship with the master that he was a frequent visitor, as we saw on inspection of the visitors' log maintained in the Porters' Lodge.

'Now, Oliver was hard of hearing. He had difficulty seeing without his glasses, although he clung to the fiction he only needed them for reading. He needed to take frequent breaks because of his age and the amount of coffee he drank. Whoever did this, whoever killed the master, took advantage of having that rather intimate knowledge. That much we knew, or at least suspected.

'But that knowledge hardly narrowed down the list of suspects. Almost everyone in the college would know about the night porter's walking and hearing difficulties and, when it suited them, take advantage of the situation. That would generally be the undergraduates who could come and go more or less as they pleased. Especially the sky-walkers and the night-climbers. Word would have got around.

'A second clue to the murder, of course, was the missing painting. It would have been a simple thing for Ambrose to transport the painting of most interest to him to his museum, or to his house, for further examination. It was a small painting, and he only needed a small satchel or backpack to carry it in. To do this, though, he had to get around the master, who was adamant that the item not be tested.'

'Because he was worried it would lead back to his uncle and his stealing the painting from the Monuments Men during World War II,' said Sergeant Fear. 'He wouldn't want the world to know the truth behind the valuable masterpiece, or have it verified to be sure.'

'No. And the reasons for that I'll get to in a minute.'

Sergeant Fear persisted. 'And when you come down to it, who wouldn't want the money for it if it was worth so much?'

'Again, we'll get to that. So, on the night of the murder, Ambrose waits until the porter is distracted and then enters the college gates and walks through into First Court. He was aware of the cameras and knows how to dodge them. It really was the laxest security imaginable, but Hardwick College never had any crimes – no break-ins, no major thefts. None. No thievery, no fistfights, nothing. It was a well-behaved college, if I may put it that way.

'Ambrose must have alerted the master to his arrival ahead of time – arranged a meeting with him – because no one heard any pounding at the door. They wouldn't necessarily, anyway, at that time of night. That was a risk he couldn't take, though. I believe the master was expecting him.'

'So late at night?'

'The master still wearing a suit at that time of night suggests he expected a visitor. Which means the ruse to get the master to stay up late had to be something important, something he would care deeply about, be excited about.'

'What?'

'A newly discovered work of art, of course. Ambrose may have concocted a story about another new find. That's what the master lived for, after all. Anything else, to his mind, could probably have waited until the next day.'

'Oh, surely . . . what if he was being blackmailed? That would get his attention.'

'As a matter of fact, he was, just not on the night in question. And not by Ambrose.'

'What?'

'I'll get to all that. Hear me out.'

Sergeant Fear sighed. 'Very well.'

At seeing Fear's expression, St. Just relented. 'By Rufus, of course.'

'Rufus Penn? What do you mean, of course?'

'Not for money. Rufus had money. He wanted a hold over the master. People like Rufus like having power over people. He's a manipulator, in the mould of people who run cults – look what he did to Peyton, what he talked her into.'

'What did he hope to get out of the master?'

'We won't know until Rufus decides to tell us. He may have just been in it for the game, for the challenge. Maybe he wanted him to be his special supervisor or, failing that, to write him a reference when he graduated that would open any door he chose at any university, at any art museum.'

'With you so far. I can see Rufus doing that.'

'Through his grandfather, Rufus knew the master's uncle was a thief. A rare name like Rascallian made it a near certainty. I believe he had threatened to tell the world what he knew. He hoped to bluff it out with the master, who knew his uncle Finneas must have stolen it during the "treasure hunt" at the chaotic end of the war. The master was too honourable a man to pretend he didn't know the painting was first stolen from victims of the Holocaust. And he didn't want the memory of his uncle or his aunt tarnished. The family name was at stake. Perhaps with Peyton in the picture, that meant more to him than ever before. What Rufus was demanding created a dilemma for the master – it must be a horrible thing, to be blackmailed. One would come to hate the blackmailer beyond reason, don't you think?'

Fear nodded.

'Anyway, Sir Flyte didn't trust Rufus not to tell the world the sordid story, no matter what he did, really. Perhaps Rufus had gone so far as to demand the painting itself, and the master might have given it to him on condition he never reveal where it came from. But he couldn't bring himself to do it. Give such a beautiful thing to such a rogue? Never.'

'So Rufus sent the girl to steal the painting? I get it,' said Fear. 'She wouldn't know about this conversation between Rufus and the master. She only knew Rufus wanted that painting. When he told her the idea was to return the object to its rightful owners, it became a just cause in her eyes. Yes. I see . . .'

'Now, let us turn our attention to Ambrose Nussknacker. Most small museums like his are hanging by a thread, decimated by the pandemic closings, and he needed to get his hands on the painting before the master hid it or disposed of it somehow. He never understood the master's reluctance to have it examined, but he understood that reluctance was real, and he was very worried that the painting might just disappear. He wanted above all to get his hands on that painting.'

'The Rembrandt.'

'Of course, the Rembrandt. The other paintings were basically worthless. Sir Flyte's uncle made a clumsy attempt to camouflage the real treasure by lumping it with the lesser paintings.

'Now, Ambrose might've been able to talk the master into getting those lesser paintings scanned to make sure they weren't hiding some rare treasure that had been overpainted, but the portrait of the girl? Despite the heavy dark glaze, Ambrose was sure it was the real thing. Or, in the way Ambrose's mind worked, it could be passed off as the real thing. It's a very fine line in this business, I am learning. As Ambrose himself told me, people see what they want to believe.

'Ambrose could never display the painting in his own gallery, of course. There'd be too many questions, and a ton of unwanted publicity. He wouldn't survive that level of scrutiny. But once he'd had it authenticated, he would sell it. Anonymously, through a third party acting as a front or a cover. It's done all the time by people with the right connections. Or should I say, the wrong connections.

'He would have to pretend it came into his hands legally, and the master's odd behaviour on that score played right into his hands. There had been little publicity about it apart from the small and rather misleading article in the local press.'

'How did that article come about again, exactly?'

'Ambrose told the reporter after his first visit to the master, days before he was murdered. Gave him the scoop. His first thought had been to force the master's hand. But the master still wouldn't budge. No one else had seen the painting, remember.'

'Except for the reporter who had seen Nussknacker's photos, I thought.'

'He did, but remember they proved nothing and could not be used for valuation. The quality was too poor. He couldn't progress any further with the story.

'Again, it was all a feint to force the master's hand, to make him fear a better image might leak out, inviting the gaze of the entire world of social media. When the ruse failed, Ambrose realized that stealing the painting would mean he got to keep it, to sell it, to keep all the money for it. It took him a while to get there, to give him some credit. Stealing wasn't his first thought, but I believe one look at his finances will show the pressure he was under. He realized he had to have that painting. And he had to have it by any means available to him.'

'Including murder.'

'When it came right down to it, including murder, but I believe he thought he could simply steal it without the master's noticing at first or wanting to make a fuss. Remember, the master kept saying it was worthless, so Ambrose thought that meant he wasn't keeping close tabs on it. If he really thought it worthless – perhaps the master was getting past it, might have been Ambrose's reasoning – months might go by until he noticed it was gone. Even if he suspected Ambrose of having a hand in its theft, the master probably couldn't prove it.

'Luckily for the police, the first step Ambrose took was to get an image validated by an established authority, to verify that he was right about it. I might add that top-notch online research by a member of our team took us where we needed to be. Ambrose took a proper photograph – one he didn't show to the newspaper reporter – and uploaded it to the website of Galvestone's, among the world's renowned experts in the art world. What he didn't know was that there existed at the time a security flaw. It was quickly fixed, but the flaw showed the precise GPS coordinates of the person uploading the photo.

'And wouldn't you know it, the photo was uploaded from Ambrose Nussknacker's premises.

'Galvestone's have since fixed the security flaw, but for Ambrose it was too late. Unbeknownst to him, he had not only sent a photo of the Rembrandt to Galvestone's and revealed its exact location, he had displayed that information for anyone to see online. More than a few subscribers to the website took . . . what are they called, screenshots?'

Sergeant Fear nodded.

'Screenshots showing Ambrose's accidentally revealed location. He was hoping for anonymity, but he got famous.'

'I could almost feel sorry for Ambrose Nussknacker,' said Fear. 'But I don't. Do you think he planned this? Like, days in advance?'

'No. He acted quickly and instinctively and ruthlessly. It must have seemed to him like a miracle – the answer to his prayers – when he first saw the painting in the master's study. One glance at that painting told him what it likely was. But he had to make sure.

'Then, he decided he had to have it. There were too many people about that afternoon and he'd signed himself into the college at the Porters' Lodge so he couldn't do anything about it right then and there. He formulated a plan, hoping the dinner at Professor Beadle-Batsford's house that evening would serve as sufficient alibi. Later, the professor and her daughter needed an alibi, too, and he was happy to comply – overjoyed, as it gave him an ace in the hole.'

'What about that "slight" figure that Oliver thought he saw about the relevant time in the academic robe, headed for the Master's Lodge?'

'I would be surprised if that weren't Patricia, wearing the gown her daughter wore to matriculation. Patricia, no doubt come to talk to the master at last about their daughter. She must just have missed running into Ambrose.'

'You don't think she killed the master?'

'I don't. I think Sir Flyte was alive when she got there. He must have had to hustle her straight out, telling her they would talk soon, he had another appointment just then – which was nothing but the truth. We'll get that gown tested for blood spatter if need be, but I don't think killing him would gain her anything. Ambrose is another matter. He sneaked into the college after dropping Rufus off.'

'Surely that will show up in the security footage around King's Parade.'

'It doesn't show anything but him dropping Rufus off and driving away. He didn't come back by King's Parade. He drove to his gallery, parked his car in his usual spot in the car park there, changed his clothes and then rode his bicycle back to Hardwick.'

'He was shown on camera pedalling to the college?'

'I had officers check CCTV for a mid-sized man perhaps wearing a hoodie and jeans and a face mask. Or something dark and anonymous, like a tracksuit. The usual student – or burglar – garb. He changed his clothes at the gallery. In fact, police searching the gallery took photos, which I had emailed to me. The building holds an office and exhibit space where a few local artist pieces are sold on consignment. The photos show dark running clothes hanging on a peg behind the door of his office.'

'You might have mentioned all this, guv.'

'Not until I was sure, and the clothing alone wasn't solid enough evidence. Anyway, the CCTV has already shown us a bicycle left on Bene't Street and someone in a hoodie retrieving it around the time we think the murder was committed. It's not definitive and there are hundreds of rides in the city at any given moment, but they're examining the footage of the bicycle. If we can get the bike's details, we've got him.'

'OK. Walk me through every step. How did he think he'd get away with it?'

'He returns to the college, arriving after Rufus has left for the pub and Patricia has been shooed away, and waits in the shadows for the porter to settle into his sitting room. Once past the Porters' Lodge, he ducks into the shadows again and waits for the camera to move out of range. He makes a sprint for the Master's Lodge, where he keeps his prearranged meeting. This time, though, he's pretending he has a work of art he wants the master to see. He needs a pretext. So in his backpack he's carrying a painting or an artifact of some kind. My guess is it's one of the many items we'll find in the master's office. If we find fingerprints on it belonging to Ambrose, I don't know how conclusive that will be, but it will be a start in connecting the dots in this scenario.'

'I'm with you so far, sir,' said Sergeant Fear. 'So Ambrose hangs around until nearly midnight, and then kills the master when the bells start ringing? No, wait—'

'Not midnight, no. He kills him at around eleven thirty, definitely before midnight, and then leaves. The scream was from the person who found the body. From Peyton. Doing what she was sent to do: steal the painting for her boyfriend.'

'I still don't understand why she would do that.'

St. Just turned his hands palms-up in a 'who knows?' gesture.

'Have you ever been young and in love? In a nearly obsessive way? Would you be willing to do anything to save or please your loved one?' He'd asked himself that question. Where was the line he'd cross to save Portia? He could only hope he'd never have to find out.

'I suppose I would do just about anything for my child,' said Fear. 'I can't really say what I'd do – if there are any limits there. My wife is my world, too, but I'm not stealing for her, not going to prison for her.'

'Yes, I can quite believe that's not in your nature, but it was in Peyton's. She was determined to have Rufus. He held out hope to this besotted girl that this was the way she could have him on a permanent basis. I can just hear him asking her to "prove her love". So she did what she was told, or rather what he persuaded her to do – gently, smoothly, making it sound like a lark as well as a worthy cause. He planted the cat burglar idea in her head and, being rather taken with the idea, that's what she did. Her bad luck was that when she showed up at midnight, the master – her father, although she doesn't know that – was dead.'

'And the porter, hearing the scream, comes along, sees the body, knows the master is dead, and goes to call it in.'

'Yes. But before he arrives, Peyton has had a quick search for the painting and comes up empty-handed.'

'We believe her, do we?'

'We do now. I'll explain in a minute. Anyway, Peyton gets away with no suspicion falling on her. She leaves the Master's Lodge and—'

'How?'

'Out the same way she came in, of course. Via the attic window and over the rooftops.'

'Oh.'

'She would be familiar with climbing about the college roofs from her time there. We have to remember, her mother was a member of the college, so even without Rufus's advice, she probably knew her way around. The CCTV cameras don't cover the rooftops. She was free to come and go as she pleased.'

'Girls were different in my day.'

'I'm not so sure that's true, Sergeant. Anyway, this was all a lark to her, the midnight break-in. It was an adventure right up to the point where she found the body. She'd seen enough crime shows to know she'd be implicated. She had no business being there in the first place, no doubt dressed head to toe in black. So she panicked, and fled – back the way she came.'

'Over the roof to Rufus's rooms.'

'Exactly.'

TWENTY-FIVE
Untied

An hour later, St. Just and Fear were back at HQ. St. Just was at his desk, just putting down the phone.

'So Rufus didn't really do anything?' Sergeant Fear sounded disappointed.

'He didn't kill the master, but he was very much involved in everything that happened.'

'With Peyton.'

'Exactly. I believe it all kicked off in the professor's garden the night of the dinner party.

'We know from finding his footprints and the matching soil transferred to his shoes that the master was lurking about the garden of Professor Beadle-Batsford. He was there in the undignified capacity of keeping an eye on his daughter, Peyton. Longing to talk to her, to be a part of her life, but quite unable to work up the courage to approach her. Not knowing what to do. Should he leave her alone? Should he stay out of her life? Think what a shock to the system this very recent news was for him. He wasn't a man with a great deal of experience in dealing with human emotion. He was, however, drawn to its portrayal in the arts. Perhaps he found it safer that way – experiencing the messiness of being alive, but at one remove.

'So, the master was outside the house spying on his daughter until he returned to Hardwick College the night he was murdered. He had recently discovered some papers in his aunt's estate that showed Peyton's relationship to him. Peyton had uploaded her DNA to 23Skidoo, a genealogy website. She was searching for her father, and the closest DNA match was the master's uncle. But the site did not reveal his name.'

'This was all in the contents of that briefcase the master got from his aunt.'

'Right. There were two separate 23Skidoo accounts, one

for the aunt and one for the uncle, both sharing the same email address, which happened to be the aunt's. The aunt – Beatrice – chose to print out those pages showing the relationship of her husband to the girl but kept it a secret. Perhaps she misunderstood the link and assumed her husband had cheated on her, not realizing that Finneas was the girl's uncle.'

'Peyton was his great-niece.'

'Right. Or perhaps she knew exactly what it meant and decided discretion was called for. When the master came across these 23Skidoo papers among her belongings, he immediately understood what they meant.

'The master, smitten at his age with the idea of having been a father all along, resorted rather desperately to spying on his own daughter. With her having left the college, he had missed the opportunity of daily interaction with her. All he yearned for now was to see her happy and healthy. In fact, he may have been planning to muster the courage to approach her the night he was murdered, but the presence of other people in the house deterred him. He left, but not before leaving footprints in the flowerbed.

'We know he spent the earlier part of the evening at King's College. He was seen at a local pub having a drink alone at around six thirty, before the college dinner. Atypical, perhaps, but then he had a lot on his mind. He then attended the dinner, where he also was seen alive and well by many. This accounted for much of his time away.

'Initially, we thought he'd been at King's College until just before ten, and then walked home to his lodge, but that was not the case. In fact, he skipped the after-dinner drinks in the SCR to go to Patricia's house. Rather pathetically, this dignified man was standing outside her dining room and kitchen windows, spying on his daughter as she prepared and served the meal for her mother, Rufus, and Ambrose.

'He stood there no doubt deciding how and when to approach her, as I've said. But then he was joined by two other people. He had to duck and hide when Ambrose Nussknacker and Rufus Penn went outside to smoke their cigars. Rufus told us it was then that Ambrose mentioned a bit of conflict he was having with the master.'

'A clash of views, he called it.'

'Right. He suggested, Rufus did, that the police talk to Ambrose about this conflict. I resisted this idea simply because it came from Rufus. I thought he was trying to land Ambrose in trouble. That's my fault. I didn't follow up and insist on his telling me exactly what was said.'

'What exactly did the master overhear? Do we even know?'

'When questioned earlier by our team, the two men gave different versions. Rufus stuck to his "clash" story and told us to ask Ambrose. Ambrose, when asked, denied that anything significant had been said. Claimed it was just the usual after-dinner talk. But I think they discussed the painting, the potential Rembrandt. Of course they did – nothing else fits what happened next. I wouldn't be surprised if Ambrose tried to finagle Rufus into stealing the painting, telling him it would just be for long enough to get an evaluation done and then he'd return it somehow.'

'Why would Rufus not tell us this in the first place?' asked Fear. 'He was awfully busy trying to get Ambrose in trouble. Why not mention that he had been trying to persuade Rufus to steal a painting possibly worth millions?'

'Exactly,' said St. Just.

'Exactly what, sir?'

'Rufus was already a few steps ahead of Ambrose and had plans for that painting to disappear that very night. Of course, he didn't mention this to Ambrose, but just let things unfold as he had planned them to unfold. What he could not have anticipated, though, was the master's being killed. He had nothing to do with that. But once it happened, I suspect he did wonder about Ambrose – he wondered quite a bit. He didn't know what to do.

'Telling the story of the proposed theft, of the suggestion coming from Ambrose that he steal the painting, seemed to land Rufus deep in a murder plot. He didn't want that. I don't suppose he would have minded Peyton getting into trouble, but . . . Anyway, the painting goes missing, to all outward appearances. Peyton says it wasn't there when she went to steal it.'

'And where does that leave us?'

'It leaves us with the fact that the master was killed that night over a painting that wasn't there. But I think this is what happened.'

He paused, pulling his thoughts together. Sergeant Fear leaned forward.

'Are you going to tell me?'

St. Just answered softly, as if from a distance, as if he could see the two men standing before him, talking with each other in the garden.

'They discussed the painting, Ambrose and Rufus. I mean, really discussed it and its potential value. I think they both knew it was almost certainly the real McCoy.

'Ambrose tried to talk Rufus into stealing it so he could appraise it, offering to pay him for his trouble, figuring students were always broke. A bit of a miscalculation there, of course. Rufus comes from quite a wealthy family. Money doesn't motivate him. Success in his chosen field does.'

'Aren't those the same things?'

St. Just shrugged. 'Only if you equate success with money, and most people do, but again, Rufus had all the money he needed. Anyway, what Ambrose couldn't know was that Rufus was already planning to steal the painting. Or rather, have it stolen.'

'Right. And of course, Rufus kept that to himself.'

'Yes. But meanwhile, the master overhears this discussion of the painting as likely to be a real Rembrandt. He'd been hoping to avoid this. But now he knows Ambrose is trying to steal it or get someone to steal it for him. So what does he do?'

'Hide it?'

'Exactly. On his return to the college, the first thing he would do would be to try to get rid of the painting. To *hide* it.'

'So it was Ambrose who stole it, after all? He threatened the master into revealing the hiding place?'

'No,' For the moment, St. Just would say no more. Then: 'Think, Sergeant.' Fear hated it when he did this, but he knew he would only have to wait patiently for the solution.

'All right then,' said Fear, playing along. 'He'd give it to someone for safekeeping. That's what I would do, give it to one of my mates to hide temporarily.'

'But who would he trust with it? The master was not the sort of man who had "mates" or friends he could go to and ask to hide a potentially priceless artifact. And I believe he was hamstrung by not wanting anyone to know anything about the painting at all – about its provenance, I mean. That is what he wanted to keep hidden, not so much the painting itself. He was in a real bind in that regard. So the question is, where would he hide it and not tell anyone?'

'In plain sight is what he tried at first. Like in that story.'

'*The Purloined Letter*. Yes. That was my first thought and possibly his, too. But then he decided to kill two birds with one stone.'

Fear said, 'I'm listening.'

'According to Ambrose, Rufus talked to him in the garden about Peyton, their hostess for the evening. He talked about her in a completely derogatory and insulting way. Ambrose said he was shocked by the boy's callousness.

'Of course, Rufus did not mention this dismissive and offensive portrayal of Peyton to us but the master overheard him talking about his daughter and he saw red. He didn't like Rufus anyway and this was the last straw. He saw a way potentially to get rid of him – a way that would solve the problem of keeping the painting out of Ambrose's hands, if only for a while. Until he could put it somewhere safe, like a larger safety deposit box.'

'I'm afraid you've lost me, sir.'

'Our team just found the painting in Rufus's rooms. They are a rubbish tip – we saw that for ourselves – and the bedder who does for him staged a boycott on cleaning up after him. Rufus swears he knows nothing about the painting, or how it got there. Frankly, he's in a full-blown panic now, since he was planning to steal it, using Peyton as his stooge. Not his fault his plans fell through.'

'He didn't know it was there. Seriously. Worth millions, and it's stuck under a pile of dirty laundry.'

'You almost said it yourself. But it was hidden not in plain sight, in the master's rooms or anywhere he would have easy access to it. It was hidden under a heap of clothes and rubbish no one would ever think to search. It would be there if the master decided to pin the crime on Rufus. I doubt very much he'd do it, but meanwhile, it was an ace up his sleeve. Fair play to a blackmailer like Rufus, I'd say.

'When Peyton came to steal the painting, it was long gone. The same when Ambrose came along before her. The master came back at ten, saw Rufus return at eleven and leave again.'

'I thought Ambrose just dropped him at the college's front gate.'

'Rufus admits now he ran back in for his jacket. He didn't want to tell us that because it possibly put him in the frame once the master was killed. Before, he'd only needed an alibi for around midnight, when Peyton was doing her cat burglar act. Anyway, the master took advantage of Rufus's absence to hide the painting in his rooms.'

'So Ambrose killed the master for nothing?'

St. Just nodded. 'He killed him, then he couldn't find the painting.'

'A complete waste.'

'Like all murders, yes. He killed the master – perhaps they argued, or maybe fear just took over, I'm sure that's what he'll claim. He doesn't seem to have come prepared with a weapon for his first murder, though he did come prepared when he went to search Oliver's lodge for the painting. So he had to make do, probably just grabbed a knife from the master's desk. The forensics report described such a weapon. Then with the master out of the way, Ambrose rummaged freely through the study, but he could find nothing. The master had the last laugh, after all.'

'And then at midnight, Peyton comes along, finds the body, and lets out a scream.'

St. Just stood.

'Where to now, guv?'

'The interview room. He's stewed long enough. It's time to hear his confession. But first I think we owe ourselves a little something for all our trouble. A private viewing, say.'

'You mean . . .?'

'Yes. And then we'll pay a visit to Ambrose.'

The painting lay flat on a blanketed mattress in a holding cell at the station, loosely covered by an empty pillowcase.

'It seemed the safest place for it,' St. Just told Sergeant Fear as they waited for one of the policemen on duty to open the cell door. 'Of course, it will be heavily guarded until the Brink's truck arrives from London with guards and a specialist conservator on board. They'll know what to do. There's probably a special vault built beneath the National Gallery for just such a moment.'

For security, he and Sergeant Fear were locked inside with the painting. St. Just carefully lifted the cotton pillowcase, revealing the small treasure beneath.

A young woman of surpassing liveliness. Not beautiful in the classic sense, her nose a bit too long and her face a bit too plump, but beautiful beyond measure when seen through the eyes of her painter. Beneath the layers of grunge and varnish, her delicate skin shone through, and her dark eyes gleamed with mischief.

The two policemen stood staring at her a long time, the centuries that separated them from the woman and her creator dissolving. They stood in Rembrandt's workshop, he chiding his model for not staying still, for smiling when he had told her to be sad.

Finally, the Old Master put down his paintbrush, walked over, and kissed her.

Ambrose's confession was almost a matter of form. Against his solicitor's advice, he admitted to the killing of Sir Flyte, and of Oliver Staunton when searching the Porters' Lodge for the painting. Asked where he had got the gun that killed Oliver, he said he'd inherited it from his grandfather via his father.

As St. Just later told Fear, who had been called out of the interview on another case, 'He admits that the night he killed the master, he brought along his own academic gown for protection from blood spatter and also used it to wipe off the murder weapon – which, by the way, was an antique knife he'd brought with him. By the time he'd finished his grisly task, his gown was a mess. But rather than just wad it up and take it with him for later disposal, he hit on the idea of putting the master's gown on over his own clothing. It was a bit of an improvised, last-minute disguise that also concealed the blood in case anyone saw him.'

'But we found the master's gown in his study,' said Fear.

'We found one of the master's gowns.'

'Oh.'

'Right. He had two, which really should have occurred to us. The master's bedder has confirmed he had a special-occasion gown he kept for when he was meeting "dignitaries and such" and an older gown for more ordinary occasions.'

'So, Ambrose disposed of his own gown, one of the master's gowns, and the knife – in a rubbish bin somewhere, presumably. Or in the river.'

'Not the knife. He couldn't bear to be parted from it, he said. It was a favourite Victorian piece from his museum. It's being tested now for traces of the master's blood. Very helpful to our investigation, that.'

St. Just didn't add the obvious: the fact that Ambrose had brought a weapon and his old academic gown with him, no doubt hoping to conceal a stolen painting within its folds, clearly showed premeditation.

Ambrose seemed more interested in learning where and how the Rembrandt had been found, and seemed to feel if he admitted everything he might even be allowed to see it.

St. Just declined to enlighten him. Let him read about it in the *Bugle*.

EPILOGUE

A few months later, the *Cambridgeshire Bugle* reported another find of the century.

The books Sir Flyte had inherited from his aunt – the books the master had doubted were worth as much as his aunt thought, the books Peyton would now inherit from her father – turned out to be worth a small fortune in their own right.

For one was a copy of *The Tale of Peter Rabbit*, a first edition, signed hardcover in mint condition. The book had been privately printed by Potter in 1901 after being rejected by several publishers. It was worth £100,000, according to the Hardwick College bursar, who was the executor of the master's estate.

'Wonders,' said St. Just, 'never cease.'

And the Rembrandt, the painting of the beautiful young woman of another age? Eventually it found its way to the heirs of the family from whom it had been stolen.

It is currently on loan to the National Gallery, where it hangs alongside its famous brothers and sisters.

Where once again, it belongs to the world.

AFTERWORD

Those of you who, like me, always read the front matter in books may have noticed in the dedication of this novel:

Richard Barancik 1924–2023

Richard Barancik, who died at ninety-eight, was reportedly the last surviving member of the 'Monuments Men' (and women) of World War II. You may recognize their story from the film about their exploits, which was directed by George Clooney in 2014. The film was based on the 2007 non-fiction book *The Monuments Men: Allied Heroes, Nazi Thieves and the Greatest Treasure Hunt in History* by Robert M. Edsel and Bret Witter.

As a private first class, Barancik and other members of the Allied group from the Monuments, Fine Arts and Archives programme rescued countless works of art which had been stolen or were at risk of plunder by the Nazis in World War II. For his work, Barancik was later awarded the United States' highest civilian honour, the Congressional Gold Medal.

It seemed fitting to dedicate this book to the final survivor of this famous group, and to give thanks to all who sacrificed so much to salvage a precious and irreplaceable heritage for future generations.

While the intrepid Monuments Men did exist, my story is of course based on wholly fictional characters and events.